INTRUDER IN THE DARK

AN INSPECTOR LITTLEJOHN MYSTERY

GEORGE BELLAIRS

AGORA BOOKS

ABOUT THE AUTHOR

George Bellairs was the pseudonym of Harold Blundell (1902-1982). He was, by day, a Manchester bank manager with close connections to the University of Manchester. He is often referred to as the English Simenon, as his detective stories combine wicked crimes and classic police procedurals, set in quaint villages.

He was born in Lancashire and married Gladys Mabel Roberts in 1930. He was a devoted Francophile and travelled there frequently, writing for English newspapers and magazines and weaving French towns into his fiction.

Bellairs' first mystery, *Littlejohn on Leave* (1941), introduced his series detective, Detective Inspector Thomas Littlejohn. Full of scandal and intrigue, the series peeks inside small towns in the mid twentieth century and Littlejohn is injected with humour, intelligence and compassion.

He died on the Isle of Man in April 1982 just before his eightieth birthday.

ALSO BY GEORGE BELLAIRS

INTRUDER IN THE DARK

GEORGE BELLAIRS

This edition published in 2016 by Ipso Books

First published in 1966 in Great Britain by John Gifford Ltd.

Ipso Books is a division of Peters Fraser + Dunlop Ltd

Drury House, 34-43 Russell Street, London WC2B 5HA

TO FRANCIS ILES
WITH AFFECTION AND HIGH ESTEEM

1

THE DISGRUNTLED LEGATEE

The small family car descended with brake-lights flashing on and off as Mr. Cyril Savage checked his downhill flight. A corner, a little planation of old birch trees and then the village of Plumpton Bois strewn along each side of the main road and creeping into the hillsides behind it.

'Here we are,' he said to his wife.

The car stopped with a shudder and they both craned their necks to see what it was like.

It was early afternoon and there didn't seem anybody about. In front of the village pub, a large black dog was asleep with its muzzle between its outstretched forepaws. On a seat by the door, an old man was snoozing, his chin on his hands supported by the handle of a walking-stick wedged between his knees. Farther down the road, two parked old cars and an unattended lorry loaded with sacks of coal.

The inn itself was a small primitive affair with a faded sign over the door. *Miners Arms*. A name quite out of place nowadays, though not so a century ago. Plumpton Bois had then been a busy community where fortunes were being made in mining a lot of lead and a little silver. Then the lodes had run out and so had the miners and the mining companies. Rows of empty cottages had stood derelict and the larger houses of the officials had been the same. The place became a deserted village occupied only by a sprinkling of those whose roots seemed to have sunk too deeply to be moved.

Then, during the war, the great heaps of slag and rubbish and the stones and the rusty iron of the engine-houses, offices and weigh-houses of the deserted mines had been carted away for road-making and defence works, the wreckage had been covered by nature with a carpet of grass and wild flowers and somebody, finding beauty at last in the setting among the hills, had bought a decent house there for an old song and renovated it. In less than two years the village was almost fully occupied again, this time by week-end and summer retreats of the inhabitants of nearby towns. It even attracted some commuters.

Nevertheless, it was a deserted place for much of its existence. The owners of the small houses once alive with the lusty families of the miners, now only visited them in their leisure. For the rest of the time, most of them were shut up and locked, their modern shutters closed and their gaily painted doors fastened and staring blindly on the village street.

Mr. Savage entered the inn. It smelled of alcohol and garlic. The interior somewhat belied the drab outside. Mr. Crabb, the landlord, who met the intruder in his shirt sleeves, had been slowly adapting himself to the influx of new blood and ideas in the village. There was a project in embryo for tearing down the *Miners Arms* and rebuilding it, with a swimming pool behind and a new name to match. *Plumpton Bois Auberge*. People liked that kind of thing after holidays on the Continent. They also liked foreign cooking which accounted for the prevailing aroma of garlic. Mrs. Crabb had started making meals in the evenings; French cuisine gathered from recipes in ladies' magazines.

Mr. Crabb showed no enthusiasm when he saw his visitor at that time in the afternoon. Furthermore, Savage exhibited no signs of thirst or wishing to drink. In fact, he had the look of a teetotaller. He had on his face the enquiring expression of a lost traveller.

'Could you tell me where I can find a house called *Johnsons Place?*'

'I'll show you...'

Mr. Crabb sought a cap from under the bar. He had a bald head and quickly took cold, although he persisted in his shirt sleeves.

He put on the cap and shuffled to the front door – for he was still wearing his carpet slippers – gently towing Mr. Savage along with him. They faced the view across the valley. Not a soul in sight; not a breath of wind. On that sunny day it was magnificent. A green hillside sparsely dotted with old trees and divided into small square fields with cattle feeding in them or else crops flourishing there. A stream ran in the valley between the inn and the hills.

Mr. Crabb pointed downstream to where in a patch of greenery a stone bridge crossed the water.

'See the bridge? Cross it. It's the first house on the left. A biggish, stone place in a fair sized garden. Used to belong to a Miss Melody Johnson who died about a month ago. Very old lady. Past eighty.'

'Yes I know. She was my great-aunt.'

'Oh, was she? Fancy that. Didn't know she had any relations. None came during her last illness.'

'I didn't even know she was ill. In fact, I only knew she was dead when the lawyer wrote.'

Mr. Crabb gave him a reproachful look, as though, somehow, he thought Mr. Savage had been neglecting his duty.

'I have inherited *Johnsons Place* under my great-aunt's will. I'm on my way with my wife to see it now for the first time. This seems a nice locality.'

'Not bad. Not bad. Live near here?'

'No. Our home is in London. We started out early this morning and hope to be back again there late tonight. We're just here to look over the place and then we'll decide what to do about it.'

'Thinking of selling? Because it should go for quite a nice figure. Since they did-up this village the value of property has gone up quite a lot. There's been a lot of enquiries about *Johnsons Place* already. It's commodious and in a lovely position.'

Savage made no answer, but moved towards the car where his wife sat watching his every move and even seemed to be trying to read his lips and fathom what he and the landlord were talking about.

'Well, thank you, landlord.'

Mr. Crabb shuffled off and left the pair together again. They followed his instructions, downhill and across the bridge which carried a byway into the hills beyond. They quickly found the house.

The garden stood neglected and overgrown and as Savage gazed at it, it seemed to grow more vast and forbidding. He felt a mood of melancholy and frustration seize him. He had played with the idea of taking over the place himself if it suited him and his wife. The thought of setting to rights this wilderness filled him with despair. He was a tall, spare, middle-aged man with a long, serious face, quite devoid of humour. His looks now grew harassed and petulant at his thoughts. He turned to his wife and shrugged. Her expression was almost exactly like his own, except that she was nearer to tears.

'Oh, dear!'

It was very hot and still and the surrounding trees and overgrown hedges oppressed the visitors almost to suffocation. The neighbourhood seemed deserted. A few birds twittered in the bushes and in the distance someone was rushing hither and thither on a tractor.

All the blinds of the house were drawn. It stood back from the gate at the end of the worn-out path and its soiled white façade was sad-looking and desolate. An oblong structure, low lying and sprawling, with a door in the middle of the front with a window on each side of it. Three windows upstairs and a kind of glazed trap-door in the roof. A large stone doorstep, hollowed out in the middle by the feet of long-forgotten people. There was a neglected hen-run – a wire-netting enclosure with a tumbledown shed in one corner – at one end, apparently left just as it was after the poultry had been disposed of. As Savage approached, a rat ran from the shed and disappeared in the hedge.

The two intruders made their way slowly along the path. Now and then they stumbled over protruding cobblestones which bristled underfoot.

Savage paused before they reached the door. He was obviously displeased. He was disappointed with everything: the village itself, the house, the damp abandon, the smell and decay, the solitude... the lot.

He did not complain to his wife. There seemed too much to grumble about. He was hostile to the whole set-up and was now growing hostile to his wife, as well, for suggesting the visit there, although it was necessary and had to be made sometime or other. He trudged slowly to the door and took out the key which the lawyer had given him. Then, he paused and looked back as though someone other than his companion were following him.

There was a view of the village between the trees. The scattered houses irregularly lining each side of the main road. The church tower with its rusty weathercock protruding through a thick mass of leaves. The abandoned Methodist chapel – 'Erected to the Glory of God 1852' – near the by-road to *Johnsons Place*. To Mr. Savage it was all depressing. He contemplated it with a strange dread, like a man condemned to exile from a beloved place inspecting his future prison.

There was a bell-push on the door jamb and for something better to do as her husband hesitated, Mrs. Savage gently tugged it. There was a creak of old wire and somewhere, far away, a ghostly bell pealed in the darkness of the house.

Mr. Savage jumped.

'What are you doing?' he said hoarsely as though his wife were tinkering with something dangerous.

He inserted the key in the lock and opened the door, which resisted him at first. Then a fetid draught of air surrounded the pair on the threshold. It reeked of damp stone floors, stored rotten apples and the greasy stench of neglected kitchens.

They entered hesitantly, as though afraid to disturb some waiting occupant, and found themselves plunged in cold and darkness. Mr. Savage almost ran to the window at the end of the passage and with difficulty drew up the yellow blind. A thin trickle of light spread down the long, narrow corridor from the soiled window, half obscured by an overgrowth of dead old roses and leaves from the bushes outside.

They could make out two doors to rooms on the left and right of the passage and another one to the kitchens to the right beyond. The passage was floored in old-fashioned red and cream tiles and furnished with a hat stand of bamboo, two chairs, pictures on the walls, a coconut mat on the floor. To the left at the far end, the stairs ascended.

Mr. Savage's aunt had left him the house as it stood, furniture and all, and he was anxious to inspect his windfall. He didn't quite know what to expect among the goods and chattels of the dead woman. He had never been here before. Admitted, Miss Melody Johnson had been his great-aunt. But she might just as well have been a stranger. She had been his grandfather's sister and both of them had been born at *Johnsons Place* along with two other sisters and another brother, all of whom had died before his grandfather. Grandfather Johnson had left home early in life. He had never taken to mining or the life in Plumpton Bois, had quarrelled with his father, and gone to become a clerk in a tea merchant's office in London.

Presumably his father had cut him off without a shilling and there was no account of any inheritance in Cyril Savage's family archives. Grandfather Johnson had never got on with his sister Melody either.

Cyril Savage had met his Aunt Melody once when he was a child. She had been in London on business and had called on his father and mother, her sole remaining relatives. She hadn't taken on Cyril at all, nor he to her. And she had disapproved of the rest of the family, too; Cyril's sister, since dead, and his brother, who had later gone down-hill to the dogs. Miss Johnson had been too starchy and exacting altogether the visit had been a failure and she had said farewell and departed for good. The family had broken up later and Aunt Melody had grown into a distant memory, a sort of ghost from the past.

Cyril was a bank cashier in London and was keen on money. He had made several attempts to re-establish contact with his great-aunt, with an eye to ingratiating himself with her. After all, the Johnsons had been reputed to be very comfortably off. They had owned a very profitable mine in Plumpton Bois when the lodes were flourishing. His mother's great-grandfather had, he knew, started a mine of his own, raised himself from a modest miner to a local bigwig, built *Johnsons Place*, and moved to it from a two-up and two-down cottage. But all Cyril's approaches to his aunt had been repulsed. She had snubbed him, never answered his letters or his persistent Christmas cards.

Once only, when he had written to say that he would be in the vicinity on holidays and would call on her, had she sent him a formal note. 'Miss Johnson is unwell and is unable to receive visitors.' After that, he'd given up.

And now, like a bolt from the blue, the legacy. A house and its contents. And what a house! Large, damp, rambling and shabby.

When Mr. Jeremiah Cunliffe, his aunt's lawyer in Povington, had written to him and explained that Miss Johnson wished the house and all its contents to pass to her sole surviving relative,

Cyril Savage had pictured a fine patrician place. He was due to retire from the bank in four years and maybe he could then settle there, his mother's family home. But now... Not on your life...

'You'd better call and see the place and then come back to me and let me know what you decide to do about it,' Mr. Cunliffe had told him when Savage had called on his way to inspect his windfall. 'You may find it somewhat neglected. Of late years your aunt has not been at all well and unable to manage her affairs properly. Had I not done my modest share of keeping an eye on things, they might have been far worse...'

Mr. Savage had grown bold.

'Who inherits the money, if I'm only to get the property?'

Mr. Cunliffe was a small, aged, wiry man with close-cut sandy hair, sandy eyebrows and a benevolent expression for the occasion. His benevolence turned to acid at the question.

'There was very little left. A few hundred pounds in the bank. No investments and, as far as I can ascertain, no property elsewhere. You are the only one to receive any substantial benefit.'

'Who gets the bank balance?'

Mr. Savage was a persistent man. Mr. Cunliffe regarded him bellicosely over his spectacles.

'I do. She and I had been friends for more than sixty years and during that time, I helped her with all her financial affairs. After her legacy to you, she left me the residue. It was in the nature of a mere honorarium, for I collected very little from her in the way of fees during her lifetime. Are you satisfied, or shall I read the will to you? It is quite short.'

Mr. Savage decided that he'd been swindled by a sharp lawyer and that it was no use arguing about it.

'You needn't bother. I see your point.'

'The house and grounds of *Johnsons Place* have been neglected of late. Miss Johnson's maid, a woman of over seventy, who'd been with her since she was a girl taken from an orphanage, and nursed your aunt through her last illness, left about a week ago. I would have urged her to stay until you took over, but she had made other arrangements. So, as I couldn't find a suitable caretaker in the vicinity, I had to leave things. A neighbour is keeping an eye on the place, however. I'm sorry, but I did my best. You see, Plumpton Bois was, until quite recently, an almost deserted village. There are very few domestic workers there, if any. The owners of the properties are either elderly retired people, or else residents from nearby towns who come and go over weekends...'

Mr. Savage had left the lawyer feeling very unhappy and dissatisfied. He had a presentiment that somewhere, something was wrong...

The whole interview came back to him as he stood before the door of the room on the left of the tiled passage. He turned the knob, but the door didn't move. He put his knee to it and irritably banged it open. When he stepped inside, he recoiled.

This was what must have been a ceremonial sitting-room. It smelled of damp horsehair and decayed curtains. There were stiff little chairs, a brass fender before the fireplace and a skin hearthrug which looked to be suffering from ringworm. A small Sheraton desk in one corner was the only article of furniture worth looking at. The walls and mantelpiece were littered with framed and fading photographs of the Johnson family. Mr. Savage recoiled from none of these, but from the state of the room.

A large mahogany chiffonier had all its drawers out and had been resolutely rummaged. The desk had suffered the same indignity and its locks had been forced. As though seeking a hiding place under the floor, the intruder had partly rolled back the carpet, a worn green affair, and apparently examined the boards under it. He had even been up the chimney, for there were marks of soot here and there in the room, as though he hadn't minded his dirty hands or gloves.

This was the last straw for Mr. Savage. He made whimpering noises as he paused to recover from the shock and then, ignoring his wife, rushed from room to room, upstairs and down. Without exception, they had suffered a similar going-over, but order had apparently been somewhat restored there. As though the searcher – whoever he was – had originally tried to make a neat job, but that his time had run out as he progressed.

The mattresses and feather beds in the two furnished bedrooms had been opened and plumbed and there were feathers scattered all over the place like relics of a destructive fox in a poultry yard.

Cyril Savage was almost hysterical with rage and confusion until intense hatred of the unknown intruder steadied him. Meanwhile, his wife, infected by the crazy atmosphere created by her husband, had collapsed in an armchair in the dining-room, Miss Johnson's living place, with a round oak table, straw bottomed chairs and a large Welsh dresser with its drawers gaping wide.

Savage didn't even bother about his wife. He continued to rush here and there, like a caged rat seeking an outlet. Upstairs and down, to the attics and back. He was not a courageous man, but very impulsive. That was the reason he hadn't got very far in the bank. He'd made a lot of stupid mistakes during his career, charging like a bull at a gate when faced by a problem. He would have killed the wrecker of his aunt's house had he found him. That would have been another mistake.

Finally, the only place he found unexplored was the cavity under the stairs, close by a large door, which presumably gave access to the cellars. When Savage tried to open it he found it locked. There was no key. He sought everywhere for it, his anger re-kindled. He was a sorry sight. His face streaked with soot, his eyes staring, his lips twisted in a mirthless grin. He still wore his cap and raincoat; the former askew over one eye, the latter stained with dust, oil and soot picked up during his wild search. He could not find the key anywhere. He put his shoulder to the obstinate door, but it resisted him. He kicked it, but it did not move.

At last, in a transport of rage, he took up a heavy hall chair and smashed at the lock. The door opened suddenly from the weight of the blow.

Mr. Savage paused as though surprised at what he had accomplished. He felt the clammy tainted air ooze from the black yawning cavity and surround him, rancid and full of decay. That was all.

When Mrs. Savage came-to a little later, she sat upright and listened. Not a sound indoors. She screamed her husband's name which echoed round the empty house. There was no reply. She slowly made her way to the hall, gripping the furniture to hold her up and give her some confidence.

She found her husband dead at the top of the cellar steps from a fearful blow on the head. She gave a great moan and, in a burst of terrified strength, ran screaming from the place.

2

PLUMPTON BOIS

A lthough it was not yet dark, the lights were on in the main streets of Povington when Littlejohn and Cromwell, accompanied by Superintendent Harris, of the South-shire police, left county headquarters and entered the waiting police car.

The help of Scotland Yard on the Savage murder had been enlisted almost right away and already the London detectives had been meticulously posted about events and details and had spent most of the afternoon discussing them with those locally in charge.

They had not very far to go. The town and the street lights thinned out, the road narrowed and soon they were in open country. The lights of farms dotted here and there along the way twinkled across misty fields and the headlamps of approaching cars made it more difficult to see the countryside. It was early autumn and the nights were drawing in.

Soon it became obvious from the movements of the car that they were in undulating country and before long as they turned an almost right-angled bend in the road, a chain of lights grew visible, like a long trail of stars in the far distance.

'That's Plumpton Bois.' He pronounced it 'Boys' as did all the locals. 'Not much of a place. Population scattered in a string of houses along the highway and in isolated clumps on the hillsides...'

Superintendent Harris sounded bored with the place already. To him, a man who followed rule of thumb, the case had been open and shut from the start. A tramp, sleeping on the premises at *Johnsons Place* had been disturbed by Savage and had assaulted and killed him. The problem was merely to find the tramp. Harris and his men had been hunting high and low without success since the crime was committed. The Chief Constable, however, did not agree with Harris' theory, for some reason. It had caused arguments and a bit of ill feeling, but the Chief had insisted and asked Scotland Yard for help.

'Not much of a place...'

The car coasted downhill, past an inn described in red strip-lighting as *Miners Arms* and on to a building with an open door through which a bright shaft of light illuminated a hatless, watching figure. They pulled up and the figure moved to the gate of the small garden and opened it. It was a new police station and house occupied by P.C. Green and family and the spotlighted figure was the constable himself expecting them. He saluted Harris, who introduced his companions. Green saluted again very smartly.

'I'm honoured, Superintendent Littlejohn, and the same to you, Inspector Cromwell.'

Green had wondered what the protocol might be when he met high-ups from London and had consulted his wife, daughter of a retired country police sergeant, about it. This was her advice. Say 'honoured' to the boss and then 'and the same to you' to the other.

Littlejohn and Cromwell shook hands with him and he invited them all into his office in the front room of the building.

P.C. Green was a youngish man, the father of three, who had been put to bed to keep them out of the way of the distinguished visitors, for whom, if they had been about, they would not have shown the slightest respect. Green covered his wide beat conscientiously on a motor-bike and, having married a local girl, was *persona grata* wherever he cared to show himself in the neighbourhood. His wife had instructed him to behave with dignity and courtesy, for she, if not he, saw possibilities of promotion if he distinguished himself in his first murder case.

The small office of the police station had been specially dusted and polished for the occasion, numerous files and papers had been dug-out and placed in the desk to prove that Green was a busy man, and a fire had been lighted in the grate above which were hanging coloured portraits of the Queen and Sir Winston Churchill. There was a small cell under the office which, until earlier that day, had been occupied by the local drunken layabout, who had stolen methylated spirits and drunk it. Much to the relief of Green and his wife, the man had slept off his potations before four o'clock and had been released. 'If I want you, I'll pull you in,' Green, who spent a lot of his spare time watching American crime on his telly, had told him. 'So don't leave the district until I say you can.'

P.C. Green was a large, well-built constable with dark eyes, a complexion ruddy and wind-burned from much furious travel on his motor-bike, bushy eyebrows and a small moustache. When advised of the imminent arrival of the two London detectives in his precinct, he had no idea what they were going to do there. He greeted them, found chairs for them in his office and then hoped for the best.

Upstairs, the *three* were being put to bed out of the way. One was objecting strongly because he was the oldest and reserved the right to turn-in last. P.C. Green hurriedly closed the office door to keep out the noise. Later, he settled accounts with his eldest for misbehaviour at a critical time.

They did not discuss the case. Superintendent Harris, greatly to the constable's relief, said he had merely brought Littlejohn and Cromwell to introduce them.

'I told you they'd be staying here during their investigations. Have you found them suitable accommodation, as I asked?'

'Yes, sir. I booked two rooms at the *Miners Arms*...'

'The village pub?'

'No need to worry, sir. It's nothing to do with miners now. In fact, it's quite a comfortable place. I called to see Crabb, the landlord, personally and inspected the rooms. Very comfortable with h. & c. in each. And the food's good. People come from quite a distance to dine there. As a matter of fact, Sir Archibald Plumpton himself occupies the room I've booked for Superintendent Littlejohn, when he comes here shooting...'

'All right, Green. Thanks for the trouble. Perhaps you'll take them to the inn later and tell Crabb to give them V.I.P. treatment. And now, I must be off.'

Although impressed by the reputation of Littlejohn, the bobby seemed more relaxed after his own superior officer had departed.

'Would you like a cup of tea, gentlemen?'

'Don't trouble, Green. We can wait.'

'It's no trouble at all...'

He hurried to the rear quarters of the house. It was obvious he'd received his instructions about the tea business and would suffer later if he deviated.

The cups of tea arrived at once. The modest offer of a drink was a colossal understatement. Green had a pretty, fair-haired wife, but she had a determined look as she entered with a tray loaded with bread and butter, toasted scones and jam, small cakes and slab cake and a pile of chocolate biscuits. She handed the lot to her husband whilst she sacrilegiously removed all his police paraphernalia from his official desk and spread the meal all over it. After she'd poured out the tea, Green introduced her. She said she was very pleased to meet them, she had read a lot about Superintendent Littlejohn in the papers, and was honoured by his visit.

'She's a bit of a fan of yours, sir,' said Green and laughed behind his hand.

She gave him a look of reproach and left them, saying she hoped they'd make a good tea and if they needed any more to say so. She was a bit overwhelmed by the visitors but she carried it off very well. Her eldest, whose protest aloft had died down, had already decided to join the police in due course and she was in the habit of encouraging his ambitions by urging him to do well at school and then 'one day you'll be a famous detective, like Superintendent Littlejohn.'

The three policemen set about the excellent meal with good appetite. Green was anxious to discuss the case and then he could tell his wife that he was in the confidence of the experts.

'You're mostly used to cases in London, I suppose, sir. I don't know if you're familiar with the atmosphere of village life. It's a bit different, sir. If I can be of any help...'

'Of course you can, Green. We're relying on you...'

Green's tunic buttons grew tight as his chest expanded.

'But I was born in a village. Were you born here?'

'No, sir. I was born in Fulham...'

He hastened to add:

'But my family came to live not far from here when I was three. My dad used to run the post-office and general stores in Axley, four miles away. So I know the locality pretty well. This used to be the main village for miles round. That was when the mines were open. The population was over a thousand then. Now it's just under two hundred, and that includes the farms in what you might say was a very scattered parish.'

'You knew Miss Johnson very well, then.'

'Yes. I used to make a point of taking a walk round by *Johnsons Place* every night after dark. Two women living on their own, you know. Not that Miss Johnson asked me to do it. She was quite capable of looking after herself. But I felt I ought not to take any chances.'

'Quite right, too.'

The conversation was desultory until tea was finished and Green had ceased from passing round the good things and fresh cups of tea like a juggler with many plates to keep him occupied. Finally after he had collected the scattered remains on the tray and carried them ponderously away, reported to his wife that all was going well, and returned and replaced the police equipment back on the desk, they felt they could get to business.

'We've read the files at headquarters, Green, but we'd like to hear from you, in your own words, exactly what happened on the afternoon the crime was committed. Take your time.'

Green opened a drawer in the desk and took out a large black notebook, which he opened and placed before him. He'd been expecting this, had got all his points in what he considered to be order, and even rehearsed it with his wife. And at the end of the recital Mrs. Green had solved the case and suggested the arrest of Mrs. Savage, who, she said, had obviously done it!

The bobby cleared his throat and began his recital.

'On the second of September at four o'clock in the afternoon, a passing motorist called here to say that he had in his car a lady he'd picked up at the corner of the lane leading to *Johnsons Place* from the main road. She was then in a state of collapse. She'd run screaming into the middle of the highway and he'd only just missed running her down. She said something about her husband being murdered. I was at home at the time and went to investigate.'

Green took a peep at his notes and resumed.

'She was in no condition whatsoever to make a statement. I therefore helped her out of the car, handed her over to my wife and telephoned for the doctor. Then I went to *Johnsons Place* to find out what it was all about. She'd been found near there, so I went straight to the house. I found Savage's body at once. It was lying stretched in the hall at the top of the cellar steps, sir. He was quite dead, but hadn't been so for long. The body was still warm.'

Green had much of the story-teller in him. He got carried away with his subject, grew flushed and bright-eyed and he made dramatic gestures with his left hand whilst with his right, he held down his notebook on the desk, as though it might disappear.

'I just took a brief look around to see if anybody was still there, but there wasn't. You never saw such a shambles. I thought at first that Savage had done it, but when his wife recovered enough – the doctor sent her to hospital as soon as he saw her at the police station – she said the house was like that when they arrived. Whoever did it must have been searching for something without finding it. Cupboards burst open, drawers pulled out and contents flung around, even the beds had been slit and rifled.'

'I gather that a lot of fingerprints were found.'

'Yes, sir. Far too many. The experts sorted out those of the late Miss Johnson and of Sarah Rasp, the maid, and after eliminating them, found there were still plenty to spare. The place had been empty for a week and anybody might have got inside and had a look round and handled stuff. It wasn't hard to get in. The window catches were poor simple things and the one in the pantry at the back wasn't fastened, although I'm sure it was the last time I looked round the place. I kept an eye on it, but I couldn't be there all the time; this is a big district. Besides, the house had been gone over by the lawyers and the valuers when the inventory was made in connection with probate. The finger-print men took a lot of photographs, but, so far, they haven't been of much use.'

'You had a brief look around and then, I gathered from the file, you reported the matter and headquarters took over.'

'That's right. Mrs. Savage said her husband had a fiery nature at the best of times and when he saw the place, he lost his temper and his head. He was wild about it. She said her first impression on looking into the downstairs rooms made her quite ill. She was afraid somebody was there and would do them harm. It seems she was right. She's a timid, highly-strung woman and seems to have been completely dominated by Savage. From what she said about the way he behaved in *Johnsons Place* when he found the condition it was in, was enough to drive anybody else round the bend. Mrs. Savage didn't go upstairs. Her heart's not too good and the excitement seems to have brought on a mild attack, from what I could gather.'

'She didn't see her husband's assailant?'

'No, sir. She sat in the dining-room trying to get her breath and it seems that she fainted. She said Savage was too busy to bother about her and, in any case, he'd enough on his plate with what he'd found, to keep him occupied without her being a trouble. She's that way. I'd guess he's reduced her to a wreck by his bad temper and selfishness... She said she heard him rushing about and cursing and swearing and then he must have tried the door at the top of the cellar steps under the staircase. It was locked and he couldn't find the key. That was the last straw. He seemed to go mad and sounded to be breaking down the door with a large chair from the hall. When he got the door open, there was somebody there. Must have been. He shouted "Ah" and then there was silence. She struggled to the hall and found him dead. Must have been a horrible ordeal for her.'

'And the key was on the inside of the lock, as though the intruder had fastened himself in to prevent Savage finding him.'

'That's right, sir. He hit Savage with a heavy poker he took from the rubbish stored in the cellar. It was part of a set of fire-irons; we found the shovel and tongs later.'

'And Mrs. Savage didn't go right away to see what was happening outside the dining-room door? There must have been a big commotion.'

'There must. But she says she collapsed when she heard the noise her husband was making and the way he was taking-on and she didn't come to herself for a time. By then, he was dead and the murderer had got clean away without being seen.'

'Nobody saw him arriving or leaving?'

'Not a soul. I've enquired all over the village. Nobody saw any traces of a stranger.'

'There was nobody other than the Savages seen about the place all the afternoon, then.'

'That's true, sir. Hardly anybody saw the Savages arrive. They stopped at the *Miners* to enquire where *Johnsons Place* was. Crabb, the landlord, showed them the way. The village was more than usually empty at the time. It was the day when a noon market bus runs to Povington and quite a lot of people catch it. The women travel by it to do their week-end shopping and the local farmers go about their business, too, if they haven't a car. There's a return bus at five. The extra noon bus only runs on Fridays and Saturdays. The murder was last Friday, as you know.'

'We'll go and see *Johnsons Place* first thing in the morning. And now, unless you've anything else you specially wish to talk to us about, Green, we'll make our way to the hotel.'

'The house was pretty well left as it was found at the time we discovered the murder, sir. Mrs. Savage is still in Povington General Hospital. Her heart wasn't strong and it seems she's no relatives to look after her. Her only brother's in Australia.'

Green closed his notebook and put it away and then took his cap from a hook on the door and put it on to show he was at their service.

'Please thank your wife for the excellent meal, Green, and tell her we'll be seeing her again soon.'

'It was a pleasure, sir. I'll take you to the *Miners Arms* and see you comfortably settled now, gentlemen...'

The inn was a few hundred yards away indicated by its flamboyant sign glaring incongruously in the empty main street. There was a string of cars parked in front of it and, instinctively, Green glanced along them to make sure they all had their lights on.

There were two entrances: the main one with swing doors and the fluorescent lighting of the entrance hall shining through its glass panels; the other a smaller doorway, illuminated, but with dimmer lights showing through old ground-glass panes orna-mented with the name *Saloon Bar* on each, the old hitherto unal-tered part of the inn.

The hall was empty. There had been recent renovations. The old solid woodwork had been replaced by flimsy modern highly-polished timber and chromium fittings, strip lighting and a palm tree in a tub. The dining-room was to the rear on the right; a new fancy cocktail bar on the left. The bar seemed busy, and as two waitresses passed in and out of the dining-room with loaded trays, the sounds of knives and forks rattling on plates came and went.

A closed door at the right of the hall led to the modest saloon bar, still in its old-fashioned state which had pleased the old-time lead and silver miners, but soon to be torn down and converted into a second bar and called *The Silver Mine* in memory of its opulent past.

There was a smell of frying and of garlic on the air. Crabb, now dressed up to receive guests, hastened to meet the newcomers from his lair under the stairs. Green introduced them.

'I reserved rooms for Superintendent Littlejohn and Inspector Cromwell earlier today...'

'For tonight?'

'Probably two or three days.'

'Going to solve the crime in that short time.'

They ignored this impudent quip and he called the handy-man who filled the posts of hall-porter, barman, taproom waiter and chucker-out. He looked like a retired punch-drunk boxer.

'Take up the gentlemen's bags, Hank. May I offer you a drink on the house, gentlemen?'

They said they'd wait until after dinner.

'It's already being served. It's getting a bit late, you know. The dining-room's full, but I'll find you a nice quiet table after you've seen your rooms and had a wash.'

He stopped two men making for the bar. One wore a clerical collar.

'Mr. Hubbard! Reverend Luttrell! These are the two Scotland Yard officers on the *Johnsons Place* job. Mr. Hubbard is Chairman of the District Council, Superintendent. And Mr. Luttrell is the vicar...'

Mr. Hubbard was a little, thin bony man, with a flushed nose, irritable-looking, full of his own importance. He had a facial tic which made him wink one eye at intervals. The parson was tall and fat, with a double chin, and he looked to have been poured in his clothes. He was obviously the other man's guest and eager to be getting to his food. He kept eyeing the dining-room door as though afraid there might be no room inside.

There were handshakes all round in which Mr. Crabb also became involved, much to his surprise.

Mr. Hubbard thought he'd better welcome the two policemen officially.

'Discovered anything yet?'

His face twitched and he winked one eye as though he were sharing a secret with them.

'I wish you the best of luck. If I can be of any help, don't hesitate to call on me. I live in the village and anybody will tell you my address. I'm chairman of the local R.D.C. and a J.P. I'm also an estate agent auctioneer and valuer and I get about quite a bit. So you see, I'm well qualified to supply information. You'll find it hard going on your own here. People are very cagey.'

The vicar nodded convulsively and bared his teeth to show he heartily concurred in all that had been said, and he looked sadly at the dining-room door again. Meanwhile Green stood awkwardly by, wondering what to do next. Hubbard hadn't finished.

'I didn't know the murdered man. Never saw him in my life. Knew his aunt very well, though. Same age as me. We attended the village school together when we were youngsters. Then Melody went away to a girls' school and I to the Povington

Grammar School. She wasn't popular locally. Never mixed with the village people. A bit uppish.'

'A good churchwoman, though. A good woman.'

The vicar chimed-in in a round fruity voice as though he thought a testimonial was due from him.

'Will you gentlemen take anything?' said Hubbard, ignoring the parson and perhaps anxious to be seen hobnobbing with the men from Scotland Yard.

'We've not seen our rooms yet. Please excuse us.'

'Another time, then. Come on, Luttrell. The meal will be getting cold.' It certainly wasn't the vicar's fault if it was. He bade them an eager goodnight and almost ran to his food.

Crabb led the way upstairs.

Green saw Littlejohn and Cromwell safely in their rooms and then excused himself, after making an appointment to meet them next morning.

The rooms smelled of new paint and had obviously been renovated on the crest of the wave of local popularity.

Crabb turned to go. Then he paused as though struck by a sudden thought.

'I took the liberty of introducing you to Mr. Hubbard, as he's lived here all his life and could probably give you some tips about the locality. It's said he was once sweet on Miss Melody Johnson when they were young. In fact, I did hear he was the cause of her never marrying...'

Time changes everything! Littlejohn wondered what the cocky little shrivelled-up old man with the facial tic had looked like in the days of his romance with Miss Melody. 'Uppish', Hubbard had called her.

'Funny things go on in isolated communities like this village used to be. You'll find out. You won't get much help from the locals. You see, they hang together. I've been here ten years and I'm still not one of them. If you don't *belong*, you get nowhere. I go as far as to say that if the locals knew who'd killed Savage and it happened to be one of them, they wouldn't tell. In fact, I wouldn't put it past 'em to help him get away with it if they felt that way inclined.'

Crabb paused.

'Your dinner's ready, gentlemen, and if you'll tell the hall-porter when you want waking in the morning, he'll see to it.'

3

JOHNSONS PLACE

The following morning was sunny and clear again. Littlejohn stood for a while at his bedroom window admiring the view of the distant hills and the pleasant whitewashed farms dotted across the valley. Here and there the ground was broken and still gave signs of having once harboured the mines which had made the village rich and then suddenly given out and as quickly reduced it to a wilderness of empty shops and ruined shopkeepers.

Judging from the scene outside, however, there wasn't much wrong with the place now. It had suddenly revived from the over-spill of nearby towns. A knot of women stood at the hotel door waiting for the bus to Povington. Grocery and butchers' vans were delivering orders and the chimneys of the single and terraced houses once occupied by miners were smoking and women were gossiping at the doors.

He found Cromwell waiting for him in the deserted dining-room. The place was stuffy and smelled of stale tobacco smoke. At one end the scraps and relics of the night before stood piled on a table.

Cromwell was, as usual, a fresh and cheerful companion. As he waited for Littlejohn he had been sending postcards to his wife and daughters with whom he kept in daily touch wherever he went. He said he'd ordered bacon and eggs for both of them.

'Crabb isn't up yet, but his wife offered us continental breakfast if we preferred it. I said we didn't. We're not on holidays.'

'Good for you!'

After breakfast, P.C. Green appeared, his face rosy and polished and his uniform spick and span. His wife had carefully inspected him before he left home and titivated him up a bit.

'You want to make a good impression. This might be your big chance.'

Green said he'd called to take them to *Johnsons Place*, or anywhere else they cared to visit for that matter. On the way they encountered Crabb coming downstairs. He was in his shirt and trousers with his braces hanging and he wore carpet slippers.

'Mornin', gentlemen. Excuse my dishabilly. I didn't think there'd be anybody about. Didn't get to bed till two.'

He looked as if he'd been half-seas over when he did get there, too.

On the way to *Johnsons Place* Green admitted that he didn't like Crabb.

'A layabout who leaves all the work to his wife.'

'How long has he been at the *Miners Arms?*'

'About ten years. It used to be run by a Mrs. Millett, a widow who'd inherited it from her father. She was a Knott before she married.'

'And what's particular about being a Knott?'

Green looked surprised.

'This village used to be mainly populated by four families. The Knotts, the Prices, the Tullys and the Penkethmans. They arrived here when the mines were opened and seemed to bring all their relations with them, too. Then they had children galore until the place was full of them. You've got to be careful when you speak ill of anybody here. You might be abusing a man to his cousin or his uncle which would be taken very badly. They all still hang together. It was those families who mainly stayed on in Plumpton when the mines closed. They'd got rooted here. They took jobs on the land or on the roads or water board. Even if they worked miles away, they kept living here. They still form a sort of solid base to the population. I've found that if I keep on the right side of them, my job's much easier.'

He paused for breath.

'I think you were telling us about Crabb and you mentioned a Mrs. Millett.'

'Sorry. I got carried away. Crabb married Mrs. Millett. She must have been a lot older than he was, but she owned the pub, you see. She ended up by drinking herself to death and it's said that Crabb encouraged her. He inherited the place when she died and later sold it to a brewery in Povington who kept him on as a tenant. Soon after his first wife died, he married again. A woman he'd been carrying-on with while his first was alive. She's a good worker, I must say, and she keeps the place going. Matter of fact, she's been responsible for the changes there, the renovations and up-to-date fittings and decorations of the *Arms*. But Crabb will kill her with work like he did his first with drink... Here we are.'

They turned into the lane leading to *Johnsons Place*. It looked more desolate than ever. Green had a key and let them in. The cold, damp smell of unoccupied and neglected property met them as they opened the door.

The police had left the place almost as it was when Savage first visited it. Green, with a gesture of his hand, indicated that it was all theirs. The atmosphere of the house settled on them like a depressing pall. Littlejohn could imagine how Savage had felt when he arrived to claim his inheritance. It was like stepping into an unreal world where shades of departed occupants were hanging about waiting to see what was to be done. In the forlorn atmosphere of the place there remained the slight odour which pervades some houses where very old people once lived. The stuffy smell of airless decay.

The furniture throughout was good and had once been well kept. The large four-poster bed where the late mistress had slept and died had been stripped of its bedclothes and the mattress was bare. The dusty hangings remained, faded, pinned to the curtain-poles with rusty fittings.

They walked dejectedly from room to room. The large kitchen with its big coke stove and oven, on top of which the neglected pans had left red rings of rust. Once highly-polished copper vessels hanging from hooks on the walls were black and spotted with verdigris. A half-bottle of milk, forgotten in the large sink, had solidified with age and gave off a rancid smell.

The drawers in the furniture had been left gaping, their contents exposed, just as the police had come upon them. Little-john turned over the oddments casually. There was little information there. Miss Johnson seemed to have been a hoarder of odds and ends. One got the impression that she had found it hard to part with anything. In one drawer, a score or more of empty sewing-cotton bobbins; another was almost full of tin boxes containing old buttons of every shape and size; in another little clippings of silk, wool, cotton, of all colours.

One of the kitchen drawers even held an accumulation of empty match boxes. There were large piles of old newspapers and magazines there, too, and one of the two larders was lined with shelves holding empty jam jars and useless, cheap, straw fruit baskets. The wardrobes of the bedrooms contained a mass of clothes, even a man's suit or two which might have belonged to Miss Melody's father, and many of the garments looked ready to disintegrate with moth and age at a touch.

'I had heard Miss Johnson was a careful woman and never able to persuade herself to throw anything away in case it might be useful at some time.'

'Who told you, Green?'

Green looked at Littlejohn as though he'd suddenly wakened from a dream.

'I've forgotten, sir.'

Finally, in the dining-room, where the large grandfather clock had stopped and there were traces of mice, stood an oak chest of drawers which had been closed after a search. Littlejohn opened the drawers one after another. They were filled with papers. Old receipted bills, invoices, recipes copied out in old-fashioned handwriting, catalogues... all jammed so tight that the drawers would hardly open.

'Have these been gone through, Green?'

'Yes, sir. Two constables, clerks from headquarters, did that. They were here a whole day. They took away a few papers which they thought might be useful. The rest, they reported, were mere routine. I called here two or three times to see how they were getting on.'

'I saw the letters they took away at headquarters yesterday. They were business letters. So, all this mass is useless to us?'

'They were left there ready for burning, sir. I gather that they found no correspondence with members of Miss Johnson's family. This lot in the drawers are bare business letters, like repairs to the house, mail order invoices, etc. She seemed to do much of her shopping by mail order. There was nothing at all intimate or private among the papers. She seemed to have no contact with her family or old friends. Some of the papers there go back over thirty years, sir. There are even bills paid by her father...'

Finally, the cellar door under the stairs. It had been smashed open and the police had left it as they found it. An old skin rug, presumably used to keep out the draughts, had been rolled aside and on the tiles, a realistic chalk diagram showed where Savage's body had been found.

'The whole place was gone over for fingerprints and foot-prints, Green?'

'Yes, sir. They went over the cellar, as well. Wasn't there a report on the file at headquarters?'

'Yes, but it was of little help. After the prints of those which were expected to be there, there were several others which couldn't be identified. That phase of the case will come later, I expect.'

There was electricity in the house and a switch on the inside of the cellar doorway. Green put on the light, which hung over the centre of the large vault-like room, ventilated by an iron grid, but without windows. The walls had once been whitewashed, but now were badly soiled. Cobwebs hung from the great beams. This, too, had been a repository for Miss Johnson's hoarding. Old damaged furniture, disused pans and buckets, stacks of empty jam jars, paint cans and honey pots, boxes, sacks, baskets... Over all, the damp, airless smell which characterised the whole of the property.

Littlejohn looked around with distaste.

'It's like a morgue.'

It smelled faintly like one, too. There was a drain in the middle of the stone floor, presumably for when the place was swilled out. There was an aroma of chloride of lime around it.

Green shuddered. Perhaps it wasn't out of fear, but the place was deep in the earth and was stone-cold like a vault.

'What was the general theory about who was behind the door and what he was doing there when Savage disturbed him, Green?'

Green removed his helmet the better to hear the conversation. He didn't look the same man without it. It was like putting on a disguise, except that in his case, Green was taking something off. He thumbed his chin thoughtfully.

'I'd say the general idea among the locals is a quite simple one, sir. They think the place was broken into by burglars. There's a lot of riff-raff on the roads these days. Don't I know it! They say the burglar was disturbed by the arrival of the Savages and hid there. Mr. Savage seemed to be inspecting everything, every nook and cranny, according to his wife's statement. When he came to the locked cellar and couldn't find the key, he lost his temper, shouting and swearing because he couldn't open it. Then, in a rage, he smashed the lock. It was a little while before his wife went to see what he was doing. You see, all went suddenly quiet. That gave the murderer time to get away.'

'This cellar has been completely examined?'

'No. I can't say it has, sir. The fingerprint men et cetera have been carefully over it, but all those piles of dirty baskets and sacks haven't been removed yet. To shift that lot would ruin our uniforms. As soon as possible, we're going to explore everywhere and we're putting on boiler-suits. We've been at full stretch since the crime, trying to find if anybody saw strangers coming and going to this house. We've drawn a blank so far.'

'It wouldn't be hard to come and go unseen, would it, Green? This place is in a hollow surrounded by trees. The lane from the main road goes on into the hills, as far as I can judge. Anybody might have broken in and got away without being spotted. Where does this lane peter out?'

'It ends up at an old mine-working and from there another track leads out to the main road between Plumpton Bois and Povington.'

'So that was quite a good line of retreat?'

'Yes, sir. There's a farm before you come to the old mine. It's occupied by Lot Penkethman. A smallish place he runs himself. Lot and his wife were in Povington seeing a lawyer about something or other at the time of the crime. Which was just too bad. The farm was locked up.'

'Were there any car tracks, fresh ones, I mean, between here and the farm you mention or on the path from the mine to the main road?'

'If there were, they were washed away by the rain the same night. Those old mine roads are only made of hard earth and flints and get like mud baths under heavy rain.'

Meanwhile, Cromwell was roaming disconsolately round the cellar. His neat, austere way of dressing had often caused him to be mistaken for a nonconformist parson or an evangelist. Now, he looked like a prophet of doom. He hated the cold and the temperature of the cellar had made his teeth chatter, his face pale, and his nose red. He looked at a pile of large circular fruit baskets, stacked two-deep from top to bottom of one of the walls.

'They must have grown a lot of fruit to need so many of these things.'

Green looked baffled.

'As far as I know, they've only got a few fruit trees. Apples mostly. There's no orchard.'

'They must have expected good crops for the few trees they'd got. These are baskets used for packing apples and sending them to the fruit markets. Perhaps Miss Johnson had accumulated them over the years and hoarded them like she did everything else.'

He looked again, rubbed his finger over one or two of them, and then clapped his hands together to clear them of dust.

'You're sure your colleagues from Povington didn't move any of these baskets?'

'I'm certain of it, Inspector. I was here with them. As I said, most of the stuff down here is so dusty, they only dealt with the essentials. They said they'd come back with overalls later and give the place a final turn-out.'

'Well, some of these have been moved lately. The right side of the pile's thick with dust. The left side is hardly dusty at all. I think we'll just move the ones on the cleaner side.'

Green recoiled in alarm.

'Hadn't we better...?'

But Cromwell was in no mood to argue. He pushed with his hands and feet at the cleaner half of the stock of baskets which creaked and then clattered down in an untidy heap on the floor. There was a flurry of dust and Green, to support his previous protest, started to sneeze and choke. Littlejohn retired to the farthest corner of the cellar where there rested an old metal bin marked in dirty white: FLOUR, with a tarnished brass pair of old butcher's scales standing on top of it.

As the fog of dust subsided, Cromwell, who hadn't seemed to notice it, pointed to the wall where the baskets had rested.

'There we are!'

He might have been a conjuror triumphantly completing a difficult trick and pausing for applause.

There was a door in the wall, with no handle or knob projecting. Just a keyhole, and the door was locked.

'Now what?'

He turned to Littlejohn who was still in the corner.

'Shall I break it in?'

Cromwell made for a pile of rusty iron lying on an old and dirty joiner's bench under the ventilating grid. He rummaged among the odds and ends there and produced a small crowbar. Then he returned to the door, examined the keyhole and poked at it with his forefinger.

'It must have been used comparatively recently. It's been kept oiled.'

He handled the crowbar with the skill of a cracksman.

'Remember what happened to Savage when he broke down a door.'

Littlejohn's voice came like that of an oracle from the darkest corner.

Cromwell grinned. The dust had settled on his face and his white teeth gleamed in the dark.

The door groaned once, there was a ripping of wood, and it swung open. There was a dark cavity behind it.

Cromwell searched in the pocket of his raincoat and found his torch. He shone it through the doorway. Then he turned.

'Don't go down the mine, dad,' he said and chuckled at his wise-crack as he usually did.

Green paused in his exaggerated fits of choking and looked at him as though he'd suddenly gone mad.

'Did somebody say Old Johnson was once a miner? He did a good job here.'

Littlejohn and Green – now coughing for a change – approached.

'I wouldn't go far in, Green. This is perhaps the place the murderer of Savage was busy with when he was disturbed. He may have left traces.'

The three of them stood in the doorway staring into the recess which was like a cave. The walls were of bare rock, but the floor was flagged. It was airless and had a strong, acrid smell. There were enough wooden shelves plugged to the walls and piled with papers and what, at a glance, appeared to be account books. At the far end, where the excavation ceased, stood a large, locked safe on a slate base.

'Aladdin's cave. This must have been Old Johnson's strongroom.'

4

THE WATCHERS

P. C. Green was a good humdrum bobby, but his wife was the powerhouse of the outfit. She was small and fair and given to fixed ideas which she relentlessly pursued.

'You want to end up at least as an inspector. Myself, I'm not content to finish up in Plumpton. Besides, we've the children to think about...'

She had, when the Savage case blew up, initially suggested that they might call-in her father to assist. Sergeant Bilbow was living in retirement some distance away. As far as P.C. Green was concerned, it wasn't far enough. When alone and meditating on his affairs, Green never thought of the old man as anyone else but Old Johnny Know-all. Full of ideas, schemes and opinions, most of them potty, but too idle to carry them out. When he had reluctantly entered into compulsory retirement, Mr. Bilbow had boasted that he would be spending his time in spectacular landscape gardening. Now, he raised cabbages and potatoes and sent for Albert Green to help him turn over his allotment every spring.

'If you send for your father, I'm going.' Green said in one of his rare fits of temper. His wife knew just how far to drive him and contented herself by personally taking charge of her husband's homework on the Savage affair.

As already recorded, she regarded Mrs. Savage as guilty of her husband's murder.

'I have a feeling...'

But feelings weren't enough and now they were working on facts.

When he met Littlejohn and Cromwell, on the first morning of their stay at Plumpton Bois, Green had, buttoned over his heart in his tunic pocket, a list of useful and perhaps suspected names on a small card which Mrs. Green had cut from the top of an empty chocolate box. Once or twice his hand had strayed in that direction. In fact, he had unbuttoned his pocket and was ready to produce it when Cromwell had kicked over the fruit baskets and given him a fit of hay fever from the fog of dust. The revelations had therefore to be deferred.

Having found the Johnson hideout and cursorily examined it, Littlejohn decided it would be more appropriate to make a thorough investigation in the presence of Miss Johnson's lawyer. Besides, the locked safe probably held the most interesting contribution of the lot and it was likely that the lawyer had a key.

'We'd better close the door and fasten it as best we can for the time being.'

Cromwell shut the door and gave the lock a wry look. His assault had torn it from the back. Rarely lacking in an emergency, Cromwell took from his inner pocket a large piece of adhesive first-aid plaster and stuck the door to the doorpost with it. Green watched the operation with wondering eyes and had he been the chief constable of his wife's dreams and not a mere bobby, he would have ridiculed it. Cromwell next produced a small piece of sealing-wax and a box of matches and placed a large blob of wax across the plaster, smoothing the surface with a cigarette-tin. Then, when the mess had set, he signed his name across it.

'A bank manager taught me that,' he said, contemplating his handiwork with immense satisfaction. 'If anybody interferes with the door, we'll know.'

And they all then went upstairs and dusted one another down with a clothes-brush which Green produced from a drawer in the hallstand.

'It's been tested for fingerprints,' Green assured them, as though the murderer might have been a natty fellow who had insisted on tidying himself up after his job had been committed.

'I think we ought to take a walk to Penkethman's farm along the track now, in case there are any traces of traffic left after the rain.'

'Very well. Superintendent. Penkethman's a bit of a rough diamond. But if I'm with you, you'll find him all right.'

Green wasn't swanking; merely stating a fact. Green was 'one of us' to the natives of the village, because he'd married a local girl and any friend of his was a friend of the whole community. Or so Green thought.

They left the house and set out in the direction of Penkethman's place, known as Home Farm.

'Why Home Farm?'

'When we're nearly there, Superintendent, you'll see the reason. There's a large house, sir, Plumpton Hall, not far from the farm, which it's said, was built to provide food for the kitchens. The hall used to be occupied by the local gentry in the old days, but the last squire – he was a marquis – went bankrupt through gambling and speculation. He shot himself and the place went to ruin. The village was, in those days, built on the edge of the woods which enclosed the grounds. That's how it got its name. Plumpton Bois, meanin' Plumpton Woods. They say that if the old marquis had held on to the land for another few years, he'd have made his fortune. But he died and the estates were sold-up before the lead and silver were discovered here.'

Green's face lengthened and his mouth sagged as though the unlucky marquis had his profound sympathy.

'Penkethman owns the farm?'

'More or less. Nobody quite knows. There's a legend that one of Penkethman's ancestors won the farm in a bet with the marquis. He was a tenant at the time and the only man who could beat the marquis at shooting. There was a wager and the landlord lost. Nobody ever seems to have seen the deeds of the place. But a Penkethman was farming the home farm when the marquis committed suicide and nobody took steps to turn him out when the estates were sold. There's about a hundred acres of it.'

It was a pleasant-looking place, with its fields dotted on the hillside, small areas of ripening wheat and oats, and pastures with cattle and sheep quietly occupying them.

They were already within sight of the house. It stood serenely in a shady hollow, with a stream, among old oaks and sycamores. A modest, whitewashed, two storeyed place, with a courtyard in front and an orchard at the back. The roof was of stone and green with lichen and moss. In the yard a thin little man, built like a jockey, was watering a horse at a trough.

Green kept up the conversation like a guide conducting a tour.

'They're good people, but a bit shy and nervous about their property which they seem to think might be broken into and burgled at any time. They do say that when the fruit is ripening in the orchard they sit up all night in case anybody tries to pinch it. Mrs. Green calls them The Watchers. They're always reporting to me that they've heard intruders about. Some people think they're a bit potty. They had a harum-scarum son who was killed in a gun accident. I've been told they keep his room exactly as he left it. They're suspicious folk, who, as I said, can't sleep properly for fear of being robbed.'

'Why don't they keep a dog?' asked Cromwell.

Green looked alarmed.

The answer came before Green could give it. A large, savage-looking mongrel sheep dog suddenly launched himself from the farmyard and ferociously bounded in the direction of the visitors. It took no heed of Littlejohn and Cromwell but looked ready to gobble up Green. Penkethman whistled and yelled at the dog and it halted in its tracks just in time and reluctantly returned to its master.

'The Penkethmans keep changing their dogs. They've tried over and over again to find a savage guard dog, but as soon as it gets used to the place it seems to grow affectionate and soft. Towards everybody except men in uniforms. That dog's always very unpleasant to me and Fowler, the postman.'

The valley opened out and in the distance they were confronted by what must once have been formal lawns and shrubberies, now gone wild, with shabby garden ornaments and the remains of a broken-down surrounding wall still visible. In the midst of all the ruin stood the relics of a once fine Georgian mansion, the woodwork rotting, the windows without glass, the gardens a great wilderness. A desolate house which seemed like a sightless man lost in alien surroundings.

There was a scent of wood-smoke on the air, but no sound from the farm. Even the man and the horse seemed like motionless wooden figures. Noise travelled easily there and they could hear the traffic passing on the distant main road. Crows were quarrelling in a potato field they were pillaging a mile away.

The road the three of them were travelling along passed the farm and, in the distance, joined an old track which ran from the ruined hall. A neglected carriage-drive from the house straight to the main highway.

Penkethman raised his head as they approached and eyed them uneasily, as though they might have been calling to plunder his property. He looked relieved when he recognised the policeman.

Green led his party into the yard and introduced them to Penkethman. The farmer hesitated about shaking hands and then decided that he'd better do so. He even shook hands with Green. For a moment all the handshaking made them seem to be performing a country dance. Green even seemed disposed to shake Cromwell's hand in his enthusiasm.

Littlejohn got the impression that in spite of appearances, they had been expected. Looking back down the road to *Johnsons Place* he could see the house among the trees and the soiled white gate at the front hedge. Penkethman had obviously seen them starting out for his farm. Or else, Green, proud of his share in the enquiry, had warned the farmer that they would probably be calling on him. There was a telephone there judging from the wires which led-in the electricity as well.

'We'd better go inside.'

Penkethman had a shrill, high-pitched voice and his Adam's-apple vibrated in his scraggy neck as he spoke. He led them indoors. Littlejohn had to stoop in the doorway, which seemed to have been made for little people like the Penkethmans. As they entered they were surrounded by a gust of warm air which smelled of baking bread and cooking beef.

The windows were small and the ceilings low and the room they entered straight from the yard was in a half light. A woman, Mrs. Penkethman, was standing at a large plain table flattening pastry with a rolling-pin. She so much resembled her husband, they might have been brother and sister. She was his cousin. The Penkethmans believed in keeping the money in the family.

The woman was obviously put-out at the intrusion in her kitchen. She quickly wiped her hands and arms on her apron and before her husband could introduce the newcomers led them without apology or explanations into the next room.

'This way...'

A damp, ceremonial place this time, half parlour and half dining-room. A large mahogany table in the middle, chairs all round, stiff easy chairs in the corners and an ancient piano on one side. Family photographs on the walls and in the very middle of an old-fashioned heavy sideboard, a well-polished modern telephone, like an icon on an altar.

Penkethman introduced them all to his wife. Another flurry of handshaking.

They were a strange couple. When she wasn't using them, Mrs. Penkethman held her hands clasped in front of her like an acolyte in a religious procession. Her sharp dark eyes took everything in. Together, husband and wife seemed to support one another in an unperturbed attitude which was disconcerting. They belonged to a sect of Pentecostal Wrestlers, went to their chapel in Povington every Sunday to worship and seemed thereby to regard themselves as members of an exclusive heavenly club. The fact that their pastor had recently run away with a married member of his flock had not in any way disturbed their equilibrium. The Penkethmans were scrupulously polite to one another, as though they'd just been married, albeit they had lived together for more than thirty years.

'We'll not disturb your baking, Hagar,' said Mr. Penkethman to his better-half.

'Thank you, Lot. I'll have to be seeing to the dinner.'

And she quietly left them without another word. Neither of them had enquired what had brought the police there. They seemed as though they couldn't care less what it was all about.

Green explained to the farmer the purpose of their call.

'I know you were both in Povington when the Savages called at *Johnsons Place*, but it might be that the murderer left the house and came this way to avoid being seen. That's why the Superintendent wanted to talk with you, Lot.'

They were sitting in a ring like a lot of bridge players at one end of a massive table and Green then drew his chair back as a sign that he left it all to the other three, like a dummy in the game.

'You knew Mrs. Johnson well, Mr. Penkethman?'

'Yes, Mr. Littlejohn, I did. We were neighbours for many years. The shortest way from this farm to the main road was past *Johnsons Place*. We passed to and fro twice a week; once on the Sabbath and the other on market day, Friday.'

'Did you ever visit her?'

'No. Miss Johnson didn't welcome company. She was a recluse. Living alone tended to make her eccentric. When I was a lad, she was a fine, bonny woman...'

He cast a stern eye in the direction of the door which divided him from his wife, as though the conversation were now becoming unfit for her to hear.

'... A few of the local young fellows tried to court her. Her father kept a tight hand on her, however, which was as it should be. He didn't encourage men about the place, because he always thought they were either after sin or else her money.'

'She was wealthy?'

'Her father was, and she was the only surviving child. Her grandfather left a small fortune. His was the richest mine in the village. None of the family was spendthrifts. They just let the money grow.'

'And yet, I hear that Miss Johnson left very little. The house and a mere few hundreds in cash.'

'I don't believe it. She must have hidden it away somewhere and they haven't found it yet. She was too tight-fisted to squander the family money like that. Sooner or later it'll turn up.'

'When did you last see Miss Johnson?'

'About a month before her death. She was sitting in the sun in the garden when we passed on our way to town. She'd been ill for quite a while. She'd had a stroke. It was on a Friday. She raised a hand to us but we didn't stop. If we'd stopped, we wouldn't have known what to say to her. She always gave you the impression that she didn't wish to be too familiar, in case you'd intrude your company on her. She seemed to like to be solitary.'

'She had a servant living with her?'

'Yes; Sarah Rasp. She'd be about Miss Johnson's age. She'd been with the family ever since she was a girl.'

'Where is she now?'

'I couldn't say. She went away to live with a relative. We hadn't much to do with her. She didn't come here to say good-bye when she left. She went a week or so before the crime occurred. Mr. Cunliffe, Miss Johnson's solicitor, called here and asked us to keep an eye on *Johnsons Place* whilst it was unoccupied. Which we did very conscientiously. We even took a look at it in the middle of the night a time or two. It was most unfortunate that we were both unavoidably absent in Povington for a few hours when the murder happened.'

Littlejohn got the impression that the Penkethmans were as solitary and secret as Miss Johnson had been, although they seemed anxious to assist the police. Green later told him that they made quite a habit of taking him and the postman into their confidence, because they regarded them both as 'sort of official allies in guarding their farm and property.'

'And you've no idea who might have killed her nephew, Savage, when he called at *Johnsons Place*?'

'No. Why should I? It was probably some criminal robbing the house. It had been empty and unattended since Miss Rasp went away, although me and my wife were what you might call temporary custodians of it. We were, as I said, in Povington at the time it happened. When we got back home, the police were in *Johnsons Place*.'

'As P.C. Green suggested, we wondered if the murderer might have passed your farm on his way from the house. What do you think?'

Penkethman scratched his stubbly chin pensively.

'He might. But what good would it do to know it? Whoever committed the crime wasn't seen by anybody.'

'That's true, but tracks or traces of his line of retreat might be useful.'

'I see what you mean. We, being out, saw nothing. We'd done the milking before we left and turned out the cows. We milked again when we got back after five. By then, the killing was over and the killer had fled. So, we couldn't be involved, could we? People saw us in Povington at the time of the crime.'

Penkethman seemed to think they were suggesting he'd done it.

'We're not suspecting you. Just seeking clues about who did it. If no traces were left on the roads around your farm and fields, that seems to end the matter, doesn't it?'

'It rained very heavy for two days and nights after the crime. Also, I'd no idea you'd be seeking traces in that direction. I've driven the cattle over the old road. It sur-sounds my fields. There won't be any traces left, if any, now. The old road isn't in good repair. It's potholed and muddy. We've no hired hand here and the house was locked at the time. The only call made while we were away was the postman with a couple of letters.'

'What time would you guess that would be?'

'He's usually here around one o'clock. His morning round more or less ends here.'

'And you're sure he called that day?'

'Quite sure. I remember it, because one of the letters he brought was from the income-tax in Povington. I felt annoyed that it hadn't arrived before we left, because I wanted to call on the tax office there and have a talk about the contents of the letter, which dealt with a matter we've been arguing about for months. I'm not much at letter writing...'

They rose to go. As they passed through the kitchen again, Mrs. Penkethman was laying the table there for lunch. There was an appetising smell about the place and her cheeks were red from working at the oven. She bade them good-day as they went.

Penkethman shook hands all round again.

'So you've no idea who might have killed Savage?' Littlejohn asked him again.

Penkethman didn't answer right away, but pondered the question. He replied diffidently, like a man who, although he'd made up his mind, didn't wish to push his opinion.

'This is your job and I don't want to teach you your business, but don't you think that maybe Miss Johnson, who left such a small amount in her estate, might have hidden a lot of cash about the place. And the murderer got the scent of it in some way, went in search of it, and was disturbed by this Savage chap. That's all I can think. I don't know whether you've been told or not, but this neighbourhood is riddled with good hiding places. Old mine tunnels and shafts, workings that haven't been touched or visited since the last of the mines closed more than half a century ago. Strangers wouldn't know such places, but the older people of this neighbourhood, the ones who knew about the mines, know the workings like the back of their hands.'

'But how would that affect Miss Johnson, Mr. Penkethman? She surely wouldn't have wandered out to the mines to hide her money. She'd have done it under her own roof somewhere.'

'That's right. But that's what I was coming to. The old Johnson working started almost at the back door of *Johnsons Place*. The house was built a few yards from the shaft, originally. When the mine ran out, Jabez Johnson, Miss Melody Johnson's father, had the whole shaft-head covered over and levelled off. He spent a small fortune on it. Did it to make the house more pleasant to live in and get rid of the unsightly mess of the workings and sheds. I'd investigate around there if I was the police.'

'We'll bear that in mind.'

'It's said there was a passage from the cellars of *Johnsons Place* right into the mine at one time. But that's probably a legend. Nobody, that I ever knew, went in the private cellars of that house.'

They had reached the outer gate of the farmyard.

'And who do you think got the scent of Miss Johnson's hidden fortune, sir?'

Penkethman paused and gave Littlejohn a crafty look.

'If I knew that, I'd have let Albert Green know and you and your Inspector wouldn't have needed to be here. Would you?'

Littlejohn wondered.

5

POSTAL DIRECTIONS

The postman was on his rounds when they arrived back at
the village. They therefore left over the matter of
discussing with him his visit to Penkethman's and his being in the
vicinity somewhere about the time of the crime.

First, however, Littlejohn telephoned to Jeremiah Cunliffe, of
Cunliffe, Rymers, Hardman, Whiteway and Cunliffe, Miss Johnson's lawyers in Povington.

Yes; the firm held a set of keys for *Johnsons Place* and also Miss
Johnson's private key-ring.

'Why! Haven't you been there already? The police have a key
for the front door. What more do you want?'

There were two Cunliffes in the firm; one at the beginning and
the other at the end. Jeremiah, known as Old Cunliffe; Mark, or
Young Cunliffe, although he was in his forties.

This must have been the old one. The voice at the other end of
the 'phone was dry, irritable and arrogant. Obviously that of an
ill-tempered man.

Littlejohn told him about the discovery of the hidden room in
the cellar and of the locked safe it contained.

'Safe, did you say? Locked?'

'Yes. Is there a safe key on the late Miss Johnson's key-ring, which is in your possession, sir?'

'I haven't got it handy. You'll have to wait. I'll need to get the keys from our own safe and examine 'em. Then, I'll meet you at *Johnsons Place* and we'll see what all this is about. See you there at half past two.'

Littlejohn wasn't a disagreeable man, but there were limits. He wasn't having old Cunliffe pushing him around, even if he was regarded as senior lawyer in Povington.

'I'm sorry, sir. I've another call to make. I could manage four o'clock.'

'Very well. Bit late, isn't it?'

Littlejohn couldn't very well tell him he was going to meet the postman first and that after a leisurely lunch.

'Thank you, Mr. Cunliffe.'

'How's the investigation going?'

'We've only started this morning.'

'I don't know why they needed to send for you chaps from Scotland Yard. One would have thought that this was an easy case for the local police. They're more familiar with the ground.'

No use arguing over the 'phone. Littlejohn let Cunliffe ramble on.

'The Chief Constable has a bee in his bonnet that the sooner the experts are called-in, the sooner it'll be solved. He says the trail gets cold in a murder case as time passes and it's best to have the yard men in right away if they'll come. Personally, I think the local men know the local mind and the local suspects. However, it's not my pigeon. See you at four and don't keep me waiting. I'll be at *Johnsons Place* promptly.'

He hung up without a word of good-bye and Littlejohn went in to lunch and forgot him.

Between them Littlejohn and Cromwell had decided that the ground would be covered more quickly if they divided their labours. One would see the postman, and the other the village shopkeepers.

The ubiquitous P.C. Green had, as they walked back from Penkethman's, at last produced the card from the pocket over his heart, and given it to Littlejohn. It was a sort of menu of village notables with the addition of certain nonentities, who might be regarded as suspects. This list gave names, addresses and occupations and owed its origins to Mrs. Green, who had contributed largely to it and could have added a lot more had she been permitted.

The postman was on Green's card and when Littlejohn said he proposed to make his next visit to him, Green gave him a brief biography of him and a wordy summing-up of his character as Green saw it. At the same time, Green excused himself for not acting as official guide after lunch. He had other constabulary duties to perform which his superiors at Povington would certainly not like him to neglect. In fact, the local Superintendent had forbidden him to be breathing down the necks of the Scotland Yard men all the time.

'Green's a bit of a creeper, sir,' the district Inspector had told his superior officer earlier that day. 'If he isn't told to lay-off, he'll spend all his time with the Yard men. That'll be a treat for them, no doubt, but there's work to do in Plumpton Bois. Half a day of Green's incessant improving talk and Littlejohn'll probably tell him to drop dead.'

Littlejohn was glad of some relief from Green's do-it-yourself technique and talk. He thanked him and said it would be quite all right and he would contact him again if he needed any help.

The postman, Oscar Fowler, it seemed, was 'not one of us' to the natives of the village. He'd arrived at Plumpton Bois after being a prisoner of war, in 1947, as a temporary hand. He had proved so industrious, assiduous and willing, that he'd finally been put on the permanent payroll.

The post office at Plumpton Bois was embodied in a grocer's

shop run by Miss Mary Tully, who had lived there all her life and whose father had been postmaster before her.

When Oscar Fowler arrived on the scene he was unmarried. Miss Tully had, by then, reached forty and no offer of marriage had ever come her way. There had been some shows of interest, but they had come to nothing. It had been Mary's own fault. She had been proud and haughty in her heyday and had never regarded the men who showed undue interest in her as good enough for the postmaster's daughter. In any event her jealous father would probably have chased them off. Then, when it was getting a bit late in the day for romance, Mary softened a little. With her father out of the way and the official position and the grocery business her own, she relented.

Mary Tully had fine dark eyes, a large well-made body and a passionate nature. For days at a time she would smoulder and fling the stamps and postal orders about and treat customers with contempt. Then she would change and you'd have thought she was an angel. It was in one of her smouldering violent moods that Oscar Fowler had a wild quarrel with her, which ended in a scene of operatic intensity, after which they had got married.

After all, Oscar by then had more or less accurately estimated the value of the shop and business, found the cosy home behind the stores very handy in which to hang up his hat, and Miss Mary Tully far from uninteresting once you understood her. The amalgamation of the administrative and the executive sides of the post at Plumpton Bois was a great success.

Littlejohn found Fowler with his boots off and his stockinged feet on the table.

He was a tallish, thin, loose-limbed man in his middle fifties, with thinning, dark straight hair scraped back from a high narrow forehead. Small moustache, wide loose mouth, dark impudent eyes shaded by bushy eyebrows and a long thin nose. Sun and wind had made his complexion almost copper coloured. He removed his feet from the table but continued lolling on his rocking-chair. He took the cigarette-end from his mouth and flung it in the dead hearth.

'Ahdidoo,' he said in greeting.

'This is Superintendent Littlejohn, Ossie. He wants to see you.'

Littlejohn had found Mrs. Fowler behind the post office grille in the shop, cancelling the stamps of the after-lunch collection of mail from the box outside. Instead of striking a noisy heavy blow on the stamps with the official cancelling die, as her husband and other professionals did, she quietly, almost secretly, pressed it caressingly on the envelopes. This her father, who had suffered severely from migraine and another host of hypochondriac complaints in his time, had insisted upon because he couldn't bear noise.

Mrs. Fowler persisted in the practice as a sort of *memento mori*. She led Littlejohn through the shop and a door with glass panels obscured by a red curtain.

Fowler motioned to his wife that she could go and get on with the mail, for the collecting van from Povington was due at any time. He then lit another cigarette from the one he had just thrown away, bending to retrieve it from the hearth and then flinging it back again.

The room was well-furnished in the old-fashioned oddments which the late Mr. Tully had left behind, conspicuous among which were a harmonium and a many-tiered whatnot crowded with tiny souvenir porcelain and knick-knacks which might have been won in a raffle or a shooting-range. The place was almost in semi-darkness, although it was early afternoon and sunny outside. The only light entered through a French window at the far end from where the postman was sitting, minus his coat and with his shirt sleeves rolled-up to the elbows. Outside, a forlorn and neglected garden was visible and a ramshackle old shed. The window was half obscured by a flourishing Virginia creeper which gave the entering light a pale-greenish hue.

A table stood in front of the window with the dirty dishes

from lunch still littered about it. A brass chandelier with a soiled china bowl hung from the ceiling and from it dangled a fly-paper dotted with dead flies. A stale odour of fish and chips hung about the place. There was an atmosphere of boredom and banality about the whole set-up.

'What can I do for you, sir?'

Fowler then rose, rolled down his shirt sleeves and taking his uniform jacket from the back of the chair, put it on. After Green, he was the only other uniformed official in Plumpton Bois, except, of course, Sprott, the stationmaster, who only went as far as a peaked cap and was soon to have his large station, important in the heyday of the mines, closed under the railway demolition programme. Green and Fowler didn't get on very well.

'I'm here investigating the Savage affair – the murder at *Johnsons Place*. I wonder if you can help me. You're familiar with the village and must know most of what goes on here.'

Fowler buttoned up his coat thoughtfully and sat down and slowly began to rock.

'You're right about what goes on. I could tell you a thing or two. But I know nothing of the murder. If I did, I'd have notified the police straight away. What made you think I'd know anything about it?'

His thick eyebrows met as he frowned.

'You might have been near the place when the crime occurred.'

'Why should I?'

'Delivering the mail to Penkethman's farm.'

Fowler rubbed his chin with his ill-kept fingers.

'I'm usually round that way about one o'clock.'

'The Penkethmans were out that day and you left the letters in the letter-box. You must have passed *Johnsons Place* on your way there. Did you happen to see anybody hanging around or meet anybody on your trip there and back?'

'You've been getting on with the job, haven't you? Did Penkethman tell you all this?'

'Yes.'

'He's right. But according to the local paper, the crime didn't happen till about three o'clock. I passed, as I said, about one. I saw nobody there. Savage hadn't arrived by then.'

'How do you know?'

'Crabb at the *Arms* told me Savage and his wife didn't get there till after lunch, which means about two-thirty.'

'So you just went to Penkethman's and back and saw nothing and nobody. Is that it?'

'Yes; that's right. I was on my bike. I make all the deliveries on my bike. It's time I had one of those little red vans like any other civilised postman, but it hasn't turned up yet in this god-forsaken place.'

The absence of a little red van was Fowler's perpetual grievance. He'd a chip on the shoulder about it.

'A man like you who knows the village like the palm of his hand might be able to give us a lot of help.'

Fowler made gestures supposed to be modest and deprecating, but it was obvious that he was pleased with his reputation and eager to continue the talk. He ejected two jets of smoke from his nostrils.

'I wouldn't say I know a big lot about this place. I'm not a native, you know. I've only been here nearly twenty years...'

He gave a mirthless chuckle. Locally, he wasn't regarded as important as he thought he was.

'... Which isn't long enough to earn the complete confidence of the natives. I'm still a foreigner here, even if I did marry a local girl.'

'All the same, visiting one house after another, you must form your own views about the people as you deliver your letters. Did you know Miss Johnson well?'

'Oh, yes. I took the mail to *Johnsons Place* almost every day for nearly twenty years. Miss Johnson was quite a character. But very unsociable. I never once crossed the threshold of the house. If I'd to wait, I was left at the door. Some people take pity on a thirsty postman and I get tea or beer on a hot day. Not from Miss Johnson, though. Just a "good-day" if she was about.'

'And yet, you must have gathered plenty about what went on at *Johnsons Place* over the years. Tell me as much about it as you can.'

There was a crafty look in the eyes under the bushy brows. Littlejohn scented resistance. It might have been natural reticence or a sort of official secrecy. Or Fowler might have been up to something he didn't want to disclose.

'What do you want to know? They'd never any visitors there. All Miss Johnson's relatives seemed to have died. I didn't know that Savage fellow even existed. I was surprised when he turned up.'

'How did you know all that, Mr. Fowler? The absence of visitors and family, I mean.'

Fowler pursed his lips and rocked his chair to and fro.

'How did I know? Why, everybody in the village has been talking about this murder. Enquiries or gossip at every house I've called at since it happened. I haven't snooped about *Johnsons Place* or done any spying on Miss Johnson when she was alive. All the news and details have come to me on my rounds.'

He put on an act at the idea of Littlejohn's implication of his spying on Miss Johnson. He jerked his head about as though indicating to someone or other that he was put out.

'Was your opinion shared by the rest of the village?'

'What do you mean? I've not expressed any particular opinion about Miss J., have I? Just said she was a recluse.'

'Let's put it this way, then; if you didn't gather much information about her first-hand, did you come upon any second-hand from your talk in the village or on your rounds?'

Fowler scrubbed his untidy chin with the back of his hand. 'She never, in my time, shared in any of the activities of the village. I heard it wasn't always so. In her young days she was good-looking and sociable. There were more people living here then and more going on. The Johnsons, in spite of the family's humble beginnings – their grandfather had been an ordinary miner till he launched out on his own – moved among the upper ten, if you could call 'em such. Mine-owners, the so-called county gentry from round about, and well-to-do farmers. Miss J., I was told, used to dance the lancers prettily in the village hall now and then, and make the young fellers crazy about her.'

'How did it all change? Why did she never marry? Has anyone ever told you that?'

'She had an unhappy love affair, it seems. The man married somebody else with more money and left Miss J. in the lurch.'

'Who was he? Do you know?'

The postman lit another cigarette and smiled to himself.

'Funny, isn't it, how life and time treat people? Fifty years ago, the romance between Miss J. and Dave Hubbard must have been the thrill of the village. You met Hubbard?'

'Yes. The estate agent and chairman of the local council?'

'That's the chap. Thinks he owns the place. What did you think of him?'

Fowler had a cocky manner which seemed to grow more impertinent as the talk went on.

'You were telling me about the romance between Miss Johnson and Mr. Hubbard...'

'Yes. I was told they'd got themselves a house and Miss J. was collecting her trousseau, when he broke it off and married a woman with a lot more money than the Johnsons. She afterwards ran away with another man of her own kind and left Hubbard in the lurch like he'd left Miss J. She was a local landowner's daughter, always around on horseback. It's said she took Hubbard right from under Miss J.'s nose. Hubbard never got over the way he was treated. A wonder he hadn't the cheek to go back to Melody Johnson.'

Fowler drew the last remnants of fire and smoke from the fag-end which was stuck to his upper lip and he detached it and flung it away.

'Queer, isn't it? Time made a wreck of them all. The once beautiful Miss Johnson ended-up with half her face paralysed after a stroke. One half of it was like a mask that had slipped and was frozen, and the other old and sad. Hubbard drinks like a fish and has D.T.S now and then. And the former Mrs. Hubbard, the once dazzling local aristocrat what had Hubbard eating out of her hand, well... He divorced her and the man she ran off with couldn't some way square his conscience and left her and became a monk. She now lives in her old home at Dottering Hall, but she can't enjoy its beauty because she's blind and has to be towed around in a wheel chair after a riding accident. She's now an ugly, old evil bag of bones, they tell me. All very romantic, eh? I wonder how you and me will end up.'

Fowler seemed to be enjoying his narrative, which he punctuated with chuckles and shouts. Finally, he subsided and dragged himself to his feet lazily and put on his cap, which had been lying on the table among the dirty dishes.

'I must be off. Got to empty the boxes in outlying parts. If I'd my way, I'd close them boxes and make the people come to the village to post their letters. Sometimes, there's only one letter to collect and I've to bike there and back nearly three miles in all, to get it...'

'How did Miss Johnson finally meet her death?'

The postman raised his thick eyebrows and opened his lips like a fish.

'You're like a terrier, Super, the way you worry on. Hadn't you better ask Dr. Garnett that question? He lives just across the road and if he wasn't well-off, there'd be no doctor in this village and people would have to use the ones in Povington. As to your question, Miss Johnson's death certificate wasn't produced to me, you know. They tell me, though, that it was another stroke finished her off. It had been expected... Anythin' else?'

'Just one more question. She had a housekeeper?'

'That's right. Sarah Rasp. What about her?'

'Where did she go after Miss Johnson's death?'

'Frinton-on-Sea to her sister's. A real old baggage, she was. She used to take letters from me between a finger and thumb as though they was infected with the cholera or something. She'd no other relatives, they say...'

'Have you the full address for sending on letters?'

'Yes. But you'll get nothing from her. It'll be a wasted trip if you go. She left Plumpton before this murder.'

'The address?'

'Right. If you must. Care of Mrs. Higgins, 142b, Jubilee Parade, Frinton-on-Sea. Got it?'

'Yes, thanks. And now I must be off.'

'S'long,' said Fowler and left him to let himself out.

In the shop. Mrs. Fowler had tied up the mail in a large bag and was attaching lead seals to the string. She was humming to herself and seemed quite content. She bade him a cheery good-afternoon.

Littlejohn wondered how she kept so happy with such a bitter idler of a husband.

6

THE PRIDE OF THE MURPHIES

Cromwell entered the village stores and the jangling bell, hanging over the door on a long steel spring, brought Mrs. Murphy from the room behind an opaque glass door with a Judas peephole in the middle.

The Murphy family were not of the blood, but well established in Plumpton. Early in the history of the mines, Michael Murphy, an immigrant Irish miner from Kerry, had been killed by a mismanaged charge of gunpowder. The meagre *ex-gratia* payment by the mining company to his widow and five children had been supplemented by a subscription list which had raised sufficient cash to enable his relict, a busy enterprising woman, to purchase the tumbledown business of the local stores. It had been in Murphy hands ever since.

The present incumbent, Mrs. Ted Murphy, a widow, was a small jaundiced woman with the looks of a gipsy and a streak of grey hair scraped back into a topknot. She had piercing dark eyes, a thin mouth, and a sharp nose, all developed in the course of her business. She habitually wore black. She was there like a jack-in-the-box, and in action before the shop bell had ceased to jangle. She dispensed her wares with vigorous greedy hands.

The stores was the centre and hotbed of local gossip and the women of the village directed public opinion there, prompted by Mrs. Murphy, who during the days of rationing had seized the reins of local power and never let them go. With a word or a gesture she could damp down or exaggerate a remark, inflame minor troubles, obscure others. She was a vain woman whose four girls had married and gone away, leaving her with an only son, grown up and weak in his wits.

Mrs. Murphy knew who Cromwell was before he introduced himself. She was prepared to give him a poor reception and short shrift, for news had already reached her that Littlejohn was in the post office.

There was no love lost between the Murphy family and the Fowlers. The establishment of a complete and official post office had been a bitter blow to the Murphies, who had merely a licence to sell stamps, but the gradual addition of groceries to the official postal stock-in-trade by the late Hickory Tully had been the last straw. Mrs. Murphy's many informants kept her in touch with the comings and goings in the village and to be seen emerging from the post office with provisions was enough to doom any traitor audacious enough to return to the official village stores, to a life of second-rate purchases and left-overs and the continual asperity of the owner.

It was obvious to Mrs. Murphy that Cromwell, a subordinate officer, had been assigned to deal with her instead of the top-dog. She was prepared to be unco-operative.

'Good morning,' shouted Cromwell above the shrill tolling of the doorbell.

No reply. Mrs. Murphy stood solidly, her hands pressed flat and hard on the counter, looking ready to defend the goods surrounding her and her own dignity as well.

The shop was dark and the walls were covered with shelves loaded with every conceivable article necessary to keep body and soul together. Mrs. Murphy regarded it as an affront to be asked for anything she did not keep in stock. There was a strange mixed aroma of bread, peppermint, cinnamon and onions about the place.

'... I hear you sell navy-cut tobacco. Could I have a couple of ounces, please?'

'Who recommended you?'

She snapped it out as though tobacco were still in the black market and needed an introduction to get at it.

Nobody had told Cromwell anything about it.

'The landlord of the *Miner's Arms*,' he said promptly.

Mrs. Murphy opened a drawer, rummaged in it, referred to a price card, although she already knew the price of every article in the shop, and flung two silver-papered packets across the counter.

'Twelve and six...'

The bell rang again and a fat dropsical woman entered and asked for a pound of self-raising flour.

Mrs. Murphy ignoring the pound note which Cromwell had placed on the counter, disregarded the intruder's comments and showed her she wasn't welcome. The woman shuffled off crest-fallen. It encouraged Cromwell. He saw that although Mrs. Murphy was a hostile witness, she was too inquisitive to dismiss him peremptorily.

'Have you no less than this?'

'Sorry, I haven't.'

She scraped the change from the bottom of a drawer in the counter and gave it to him. He thanked her but didn't get down to business and turned to go. Mrs. Murphy couldn't stand that.

'Are you a detective from London?'

'Yes.'

'On the murder of Melody Johnson's great nephew?'

'That's right.'

'They're making a big fuss about it. To my mind it was a tramp. He'd broken in to see what he could find there and when he was disturbed, he got rough.'

'You may be right, Mrs....'

She didn't help him with her name.

'You may have hit the nail on the head. The views of an intelligent observant woman and a prominent member of the village might be a great help to us. I'll tell the Superintendent, who's just called on the postman, to come and talk with you. He'd have been here before, but you'd some customers in and were busy when we passed...'

Mrs. Murphy began to thaw inwardly, although her countenance didn't change. Instead of the formal inquisition she'd anticipated, here was a nice civil policeman who respected her status in the community.

'My name's Murphy. Mrs. Murphy?'

'Did you know Miss Johnson well, Mrs. Murphy?'

'Quite well. She never came in here, though. Thought it wasn't good enough, although her family were only miners themselves in the old days. They used to buy all they needed here and sometimes on tick, too. Miss Melody Johnson was too uppish, although all my stuff's first class and often better than you'd get in the town.'

'I'm sure it is.'

'She had her groceries brought by van from the big shops in Povington. Posh shops charging posh prices, believe you me. But that didn't stop me knowing her and most of what went on at *Johnsons Place*. People round here are a proper lot of gossips and I hear customers talking among themselves when they're in the shop.'

Which was a huge understatement.

Interruption again. This time a woman with bleached hair and stiletto heels appeared. She had multi-coloured plastic curling cylinders in her hair which made her anxious to get away in a hurry from the presence of a man. She rolled her hips as she walked.

'Half a pound of lard...'

Mrs. Murphy almost flung it at her head.

'Put it on the account...'

The woman tottered out before Mrs. Murphy said No.

Mrs. Murphy slapped the fingers of one hand noisily against those of the other, as though to brush off every trace of the late visitor.

'What does she want with lard? She never does any cooking. Making her own cosmetics, that's what it'll be. No better than she should be. You were saying...?'

'Miss Johnson. Did you know she had any relatives, Mrs. Murphy? This murdered man, Savage. Nobody here seemed to have heard of his existence.'

Mrs. Murphy's eyes narrowed. Her self-confidence ebbed for a minute. It was obvious that she was as ignorant as the rest about Savage. Rather than show it, however, she changed the subject.

'Funny things have happened at *Johnsons Place* in the past...'

Another interruption. A large, easy-going woman, dragging a child and accompanied by a big dog, which she tied to the door in obedience to a notice prominently displayed. *No Dogs allowed in Shop by Law.*

The child was howling his head off and his tears ran down his cheeks and nose. The newcomer seized a lollipop from a box on the counter and successfully gagged the child with it.

'A quarter of lentils, two lemons, and a tin of sockeye salmon.'

They all appeared on the counter like lightning.

'Any large onions?'

'No.'

'Any frozen brussels-sprouts in the 'fridge?'

'Look, Mrs. Hogan, I'm just busy with the gentleman. Will it do later?'

'I want them for Joe's dinner.'

Mrs. Murphy, aware that the post-office had just installed a refrigerator in competition, rushed in the room behind the shop and emerged with a many-coloured packet covered in hoar-frost.

'I'll pay at week-end. Oh... and I want a bottle of Heave-Ho detergent. The one you get a free pressure-cooker with...'

'I'm busy. The rest'll have to do later.'

'I can wait.'

The woman crossed her arms over her abdomen which obviously held an imminent addition to the village population.

'This is private.'

'Very well. There are other shops where I'll be more welcome.'

She gathered her goods, her lollipop-sucking offspring, and the dog which had already fouled the steps, and made a leisurely exit, leaving the door open. Mrs. Murphy hastily closed and barred it. Then she turned round a fly-blown card hanging from a tack on the frame of the glass panel. *Back in Ten Minutes.*

She sighed and gave the card a reassuring nod to indicate that it would do the job properly. Then she returned behind the counter to the spot whence she dominated the shop.

'You were saying...?'

'*You* were saying, Mrs. Murphy, that funny things had happened at *Johnsons Place.* What kind of things?'

'There was a child...'

A pause for dramatic emphasis.

'Whose?'

'Wait a bit. I'm coming to it. My late departed husband once told me about it and *his* father had told him. So, it must have been more than fifty years since, mustn't it? A long time ago, that. But I always remembered about it when Melody Johnson got uppish. She was no better than the rest. There was a child born at *Johnsons Place.*'

'Was that a rumour, or a legend... or a fact?'

Mrs. Murphy drew herself up indignantly and her face froze.

'If you don't think I'm telling you the truth, there's no more to be said. I'll bid you good-day.'

But she didn't move from the counter. She was enjoying the situation too much.

A woman outside tried the door and then her anxious face appeared pressed to the window-panel seeking the cause of the resistance. Her eyes opened wide at the sight of the conclave going on inside and it was soon all round the village that Mrs. Murphy was a suspect in the Savage case. It did the business a lot of good. Mrs. Murphy was soon to be run off her feet and the portentous silence she maintained about the interview at noon added to her local prestige and the fear in which she was held.

'About the child, Mrs. Murphy. Of course, I believe you if you say so. As you know, we must have the truth in a case like this. I was merely making doubly sure.'

'Very well. As you'll see if you look over the road there's a doctor's plate on the big house there, Dr. Garnett. Well, his father was in practice there before him and one night he was called out quickly to *Johnsons Place*. He was seen from here hurrying off with his black bag. It was within six months of Miss Melody Johnson being left at the altar, so to speak, by Dave Hubbard. Do you know Dave Hubbard?'

'I met him last night.'

'Tries to be a local bigwig, but I call him and his sort trash. He ran away with another woman and married her within a week or two of his arranged wedding with Miss Melody. It must either have been his child, or else he threw Melody Johnson over when he found out how she was by another man. Nobody ever knew the reason.'

'It might have been an accident the doctor was quickly called to.'

Mrs. Murphy bridled again.

'Who's telling the story, you or me? I got it first hand. You can take it or leave it.'

'Go on, Mrs. Murphy.'

She relaxed.

'Don't keep chimming-in, then. At the time, Joel Penkethman, at the farm above *Johnsons Place*, lay dying. He'd got lockjaw. He was the father of the present Lot Penkethman and, on account of his religious connections, was known as Hallelujah. Well, Hallelujah got worse in the night and Lot, who was then a mere boy, was sent to get the doctor. The doctor's wife said he'd been called out to *Johnsons Place* and told Lot to call there and tell him to come and see Hallelujah when he'd done. Lot called at *Johnsons Place*, where old Jabey Johnson opened the door and took in the message. Before he closed it, however, Lot heard a baby crying. He told his mother, who said he'd imagined it. But the tale got round and seemed to fit in with what had happened about that time, such as Miss Melody never being seen about and such like. The whole affair was hushed up by the Johnsons. They must have got rid of the child; got it adopted or put in a home. Nobody heard another thing about it.'

'And that's all you know of it?'

'Isn't it enough? What do you want? Me to tell you that the child was murdered and buried in the garden there? Sorry; I can't oblige.'

'It's certainly very important information...'

Cromwell didn't know why, but he said so to placate Mrs. Murphy, who seemed very touchy about everything.

'Anything more?'

'Not that I can think of just now. If I do remember anything, I'll be sure to let you know.'

'What sort of woman was Sarah Rasp, who used to be the Johnsons' maid?'

'A sly, secretive sort. You might also call her sinister...'

Mrs. Murphy made a point of reading most of the paperbacks covering romance, crime and horror before she put them in the rack in the shop for ready sale. It added greatly to her vocabulary of pithy words and phrases to use against her enemies.

'I never liked Sarah Rasp. The Johnsons took her out of an orphanage when she was a girl. I expect she was born on the wrong side of the blanket. She served the Johnsons for the rest of her life till Miss Melody died. Then she went off suddenly to her sister's... Somewhere in Essex or Sussex, I heard. She was here one day and gone the next. Just like her. Sneaking about. I never had much to do with her. My son used to deliver the papers there and he might have had the plague the way she carried on. The papers had to be left on a shelf in the porch behind, and every Monday, the money for the week before was waiting on the shelf for him to pick up. Never a penny for a Christmas box...'

'Queer.'

'More than queer. Sinister, I call it. She never mixed with the people of the village. She used to go away to see her sister some weekends. You'd see her getting the bus with her bag on Saturdays and she'd be back first thing the following Monday. I couldn't say more about her. The only other person about *Johnsons Place* was George Lush, who did the garden and other chores. He was a bit light in the head but he could have told you a few things. But he passed on just a week or two before Miss Melody Johnson did. He lived alone in an old cottage by the river, there, and used to get drunk at the *Miners* every Saturday night. He was another secretive sort, but the ale sometimes loosed his tongue.'

'Did he talk about his employers?'

'Not much, but when he was drunk and didn't want to go home, he used to go to *Johnsons Place* and sleep in the wash-house behind. He said the place was haunted.'

'Why?'

'Noises and footsteps in the house when all the lights were out and everybody was supposed to be asleep. Two or three times before he died, he complained that a ghost wandered round the outside of the house, groaning and trying to get in.'

'Drunken fancies.'

'Nothing of the kind. There are old mine-workings down there and wherever there are those, there are the ghosts of dead miners who were killed in the workings, haunting them. You can't dismiss those sort of things with a laugh, Mister Policeman. All your scientists and clever ones can't either. My late husband and his father before him, heard them themselves. The late Murphy's grandfather, who was himself killed underground, was often heard speaking to his family down below. Strange things go on in the old mines.'

One after another customers appeared at the door and recoiled when they found it barred. Then they read the notice and goggled as they peered in and found in the gloom Mrs. Murphy aggressively purveying information to a dark figure in a dark suit. Some thought her visitor was the devil himself. Others that she was resisting arrest. Finally Mrs. Murphy grew tired of the procession of interruptions and peepers.

'I think I'd better open the door. This help I'm giving the police is costing me a lot of money in lost custom, although they'll come later for what they want. They wouldn't dare go down the road for it. So. I'll bid you good-morning, or good-afternoon, which-ever it might be.'

'Thank you very much for your help, Mrs. Murphy. I appre-ciate it.'

'That's all right. But tell your boss – the Superintendent, isn't he? – that I shall expect a call from him. It's only good manners to call on me, if he's been to the post office. After all, I am the prin-cipal shop in the village. It's only right.'

'You needn't worry about that. He'll be sure to call in person to thank you.'

She would have liked to ask Cromwell to return for a further long talk about sinister local matters, but she never invited strangers in the room behind, where her grown-up and childish son, after delivering his newspapers, spent most of the day playing marbles on the floor or else counting used bus tickets and empty matchboxes.

'Good-day, then.'

'Good-day, Mrs. Murphy.'

She followed him to the door, took down the closure notice,

and let him out. Then she set herself to resist all the enquiries of the string of inquisitive gossips who quickly filled the shop.

'The call was official and private. I'm helping the police,' was all she had to say to them about it.

After that, she was held in greater fear than ever.

7

THE GROTTO

Mrs. Savage was fully dressed and sitting up in her room in the private wing of Povington General Hospital when Littlejohn called there. She had remained by the grace of her medical consultant and the board of the hospital, for she was fully recovered from the shock of recent events. She had begged them to allow her to stay for a little longer, in spite of the fact that the place was full and beds were urgently needed. She said she had nobody to care for her if she returned home. She was now secretly enjoying herself.

Littlejohn had read the report of the interview which the local police had already had with her. It was not very helpful or illuminating, as it was taken at a period when she was almost incoherent and muddled in her mind by recent events.

'How is she?' Littlejohn asked the sister in charge of her, a buxom, blonde, middle-aged woman with a wealth of clinical experience and a sharp tongue.

'Quite well again and enjoying herself. It's my guess she led her poor husband a bit of a dance when he was alive. All that collapsing and having heart attacks when the tragedy occurred.

We found nothing much wrong with her heart and a sound slap would have brought her out of the state of collapse. She's a hysterical hypochondriac. I'd advise you if you're here to interview her, not to be too sympathetic or there'll be more tears and lamentations and you'll get nothing useful out of her. The last inspector who called to see her soon found that out.'

Mrs. Savage had been treating the place like a private hotel, frequently ringing the bell and demanding all kinds of unusual facilities. Sister had needed to put her in her place a time or two, after which the patient had complained to her consultant about the discourtesies of the nursing staff.

Littlejohn found Mrs. Savage looking well. Slim, pretty for her age, small, dark and petulant, with painted mouth and fingernails and dressed in black with extreme elegance. It seemed that she was spending all her convalescent time in embellishing her appearance. She gave him a suffering smile.

'How are you, Mrs. Savage?'

'Not very well. It will take a long time to get over what I've been through. I believe you are in charge of my husband's death.'

It sounded as though Littlejohn were the undertaker!

'Yes. You've already told the Povington police all you remember about the tragic events. I've just called with my personal condolences and to ask if any other details have come to your mind since the local police saw you last.'

'No. I've tried to put it out of my thoughts. Otherwise I would have gone mad. You see, I feel myself, in a way, partly to blame. I didn't insist on my late husband waiting longer before we inspected the house. He wasn't due to retire yet and it could have waited...'

It was a rambling tale with little sense in it, but Littlejohn let it go.

'Your husband, I gather, didn't know his aunt had died until he was notified of the legacy.'

'That is right. Mr. Cunliffe, the lawyer, advised him of it. He said in his letter that Cyril must make an appointment with him to view the house. But Cyril didn't. We just took a whim to go there one day and called at the lawyer's in Povington for the key. Mr. Cunliffe was very upset and annoyed about it. He said if we'd made an appointment, he'd have accompanied us. If he had, all this horrible business wouldn't have happened. I wish Cyril had never inherited that appalling place. It was...'

She tore at her handkerchief and then began to weep. The tears ran down and spoiled her make-up. Littlejohn sat there, silently watching her convulsions until they seemed interminable. Then...

'Shall I ring for sister?'

The tears ceased. Mrs. Savage mopped her eyes and dabbed her cheeks and then consulted a mirror lying at her elbow.

'No. I'm sorry. But... Excuse me. Haven't I made a mess of myself?'

She restored her looks as best she could with cosmetics from her handbag.

'You saw nobody about when you called at *Johnsons Placer*?'

'What a ridiculous name! It seems when first the place was built, Mr. Johnson, who came of very modest people, couldn't find a name for it. So, as it got to be known as Johnson's place in the village, he decided to make it the official address. You were saying...? Did we see anybody hanging around? No. Not a soul. After we left the village inn and the landlord saw us on our way, we saw nobody. The first person I met after the landlord was a man in a car as I rushed to get help for my poor husband.'

'In the earlier interview, you stated that the house had previously been entered and the drawers and cupboards rifled. Your husband didn't do it?'

'Most certainly not. He was a tidy man; even fussy. The furniture had been searched and the contents of drawers, cabinets, beds and cupboards scattered about before we arrived. The criminal must have been in the house when we got there and hidden in the cellar. Then, when my husband came upon him he...'

She beat the table with her hands this time instead of weeping.

'Why did he do it? Cyril was a peaceful man and would not have harmed him. Except, of course, I'm sure he would have handed him over to the police.'

'The intruder was aware of that. I think you said your husband was behaving rather violently just before he met his death. He was breaking down the cellar door, if I remember rightly.'

She sniffed either in grief or annoyance, Littlejohn couldn't tell which.

'Yes. He was rather a short-tempered man. And you must admit that what he'd been through since we entered the house was enough to enrage a saint. The house itself was very disappointing and added to that, had been broken into and reduced to a shambles.'

'It would annoy anyone, I agree. Did Mr. Savage ever mention his family? His aunt or anyone else?'

'No. He once told me that she was his only living relative and was queer and a recluse. He had tried to establish contact by writing to her and had even suggested visiting her. But he had been rudely treated and snubbed for it. He said he had put her completely out of his mind and had no expectations whatsoever from her. He did once say he wondered who would inherit what she had when she died. He thought it would probably go to some charity or other. I agreed with him. I told him to forget her. You see, Cyril didn't need to work at all. My father left me quite enough for two to live on very comfortably. He continued in the bank because he said a man must have something to do. One couldn't just vegetate at home in one's fifties.'

'And Miss Johnson didn't forget him, after all. She left him the house and all in it. That, I take it, would mean any money and valuables in the place at the time of her death.'

'It would seem so. Yesterday, Mr. Cunliffe, Miss Johnson's

lawyer, came here to see me and to say that I need not worry about the house. He would see that it was tidied up and, if I wish it, sold. I said that was indeed what I wished. I never want to go near that frightful place again. I told Mr. Cunliffe so and he said he'd see me again about it later. My husband left a will entirely in my favour, so, as Mr. Cunliffe said, the house would pass to me, too.'

'Had your husband any enemies, Mrs. Savage? Anyone who might for some reason have wished to murder him? I know this might seem to be a stupid question, but I have to ask as a matter of routine.'

'If you'd known Cyril, you'd understand what a stupid question it really is. He was well-liked by his colleagues at the bank and all the clients there. He was chief cashier and greatly respected. He was also treasurer of the church council. We hadn't very many friends and kept mainly to ourselves. Cyril was rather a shy man.'

Crabb, the landlord of the *Miners Arms*, had, from his brief contact with Savage, described him as a bit of a pompous chap, who thought no small beer of himself. Now, Savage was cropping up as a peaceful, shy, yet popular type of man. Nevertheless, capable of violence, hot tempered, as he showed by his furious assault on the cellar door. Littlejohn wondered what his manager at the bank thought of him.

There seemed no point in prolonging the interview. Mrs. Savage apparently talked to fit the occasion and was ready to embroider the truth when it suited her. So he bade her good-bye and left her ringing the bell again to give her luncheon order.

After his own lunch and a brief report and consultation at the county police headquarters, Littlejohn hurried off to keep his appointment with the lawyer, Cunliffe, at *Johnsons Place*.

Although it was not yet four o'clock, the arranged time, he found Mr. Cunliffe had let himself in the house with the key he possessed and was pacing up and down in the hall and glancing unpleasantly at his watch.

'I've been waiting here for more than a quarter of an hour...'

Littlejohn didn't argue. Mr. Cunliffe hadn't even replied to his greeting. Nor did he ask Littlejohn for his credentials, although they hadn't met before.

'The key for the safe you spoke of over the telephone was in our possession. Let's see what's in the safe and get it over with. I've to return to the office; I've still plenty to do before my day's work is done.'

Mr. Cunliffe, although reputed to be over eighty, was still very robust. He was short and slim and had not lost his energy to which he gave vent in jerky, impetuous gesticulations. He had close-cropped sandy hair and showed hardly a trace of grey. He had large ears and a long nose with narrow nostrils which gave him a mean look, a square forehead, and high cheek bones. His eyes were small and pale, set-off by thick bristling sandy eyebrows. His voice was loud and dry and his mouth wide with thin lips. Appropriately dressed, he might have passed for a hanging judge.

The house was as unpleasant as ever. The drains must have suffered through disuse and added a characteristic moist sickly smell to the general taint of the atmosphere.

'Well?'

Littlejohn led the way. Mr. Cunliffe paused at the cellar door.

'He certainly made a mess of this,' he said fingering the broken lock.

Littlejohn switched on the light. He wondered how Mr. Cunliffe would react to the demolition of the pile of old baskets which Cromwell had neatly re-erected in front of the door of what Cromwell now called *the grotto*.

'Where's the safe?'

He'd already been told all about it, but Mr. Cunliffe never lost a chance of being abrupt and unpleasant. He seemed to be treating Littlejohn as a kind of hostile witness.

'Stand back a bit, sir. I'm going to move the fruit baskets and they're rather dusty.'

Mr. Cunliffe's lips tightened but he didn't stir. He seemed to resent being asked to give ground.

Littlejohn pushed the pile with his foot and it collapsed, raising a fresh fog of old dust. This time, Mr. Cunliffe recoiled and started to cough loudly. He needn't have put on such an act about it, but seemed determined to be unpleasant. He coughed, spluttered and clawed the air so much that Littlejohn was afraid he might burst a blood vessel and collapse altogether.

'You needn't have raised such a dust,' he gasped between paroxysms. 'You could have moved them one by one.'

The door to the grotto was there and accessible. Littlejohn broke Cromwell's home-made seals, opened the door, and shone his torch in the dark interior. Mr. Cunliffe put on a pair of half-moon spectacles and peered in. Littlejohn was at a loss to understand why the lawyer needed to don reading-glasses, but then he'd given up trying to understand Mr. Cunliffe and his ways. He wished to get it all ended and be rid of him.

'Smells like a tomb. Is there no light on in the place?'

'No, sir. I think we'll manage with my torch.'

Mr. Cunliffe stooped as though about to crawl in on his hands and knees although the cavity was about seven feet in height. He took the key from his waistcoat pocket and slowly and with exaggerated gestures of caution approached the safe as though there were booby traps about which might go off at any time. He gingerly inserted the key, turned it, and tugged at the door handle... The door opened with a metallic creak.

There was nothing whatever inside.

Littlejohn, standing at the lawyer's elbow, watched it all. For some reason, he felt a vague satisfaction that Mr. Cunliffe had drawn a blank.

'I'd be grateful if you'd lend me the key, sir. And please don't touch the inside of the safe. We'd better go over it for fingerprints.'

Mr. Cunliffe seemed to have been silently accumulating the strength for a passionate outburst which finally came like a rocket.

'A damned waste of time! Why did you bring me here when the thing was empty? It's obvious the safe has been ransacked, like the house. Didn't you know?'

'Of course I didn't. The safe was locked when last we were here and we had no key. If you had lent me the key instead of troubling to bring it, you wouldn't have had a lost journey.'

Mr. Cunliffe subsided rapidly. He wasn't used to being back-answered, in court or out of it, and somehow it changed his attitude. He gave Littlejohn a wintry smile.

'Of course. Of course. It's quite a change to get a straight answer out of people, instead of a lot of pandering. Well, let's be getting along. No use suffocating down here any longer. I'll need a bath and a change when I get back. Have to send everything to the cleaners, I reckon. My suit's ruined by the dust...'

He locked the safe and retreated back to the cellar. He gave Littlejohn the key. Then he took a plain envelope from his pocket and scribbled something on it.

'Sign that,' he said and passed it over.

Received one key for safe in cellar of Johnsons Place.

Littlejohn signed it. Mr. Cunliffe put it in his pocket and climbed the rickety wooden stairs with flat-footed steps as though afraid the whole structure might collapse under him.

'See that everything's left as we found it,' he said with a peevish backward look at the shambles of baskets below.

And with that, he took the hat which he'd left upstairs and jammed it on the back of his head and made off without another word.

Cromwell found Littlejohn still in the house when he arrived to meet him again half an hour later. This time, they left the cellar as it was and sealed the cellar door under the main stairs. Then they went to telephone the police at Povington to arrange a further examination of the place by the experts, with emphasis on fingerprints on and in the safe and footprints in the dust.

8

DR. GARNETT'S DIARIES

The doctor's house was almost opposite the hotel and Littlejohn found time to call there before dinner. He assumed that the small car standing at the door was the doctor's and that he was at home.

The square stone house faced the road with the hillside falling away behind it. There was no garden in front, just a narrow area protected by cast-iron railings and broken by a gateway giving access to the front door. There were two bright brass plates screwed on the railings by the gate.

Dr. J. B. Garnett
Surgeon.
S. P. Garnett
Physician and Surgeon.

The lettering of the upper plate was almost worn away by cleaning. Dr. J. B. Garnett, father of the present incumbent, had been dead for almost twenty years, but his son had retained his plate in his memory.

The door itself was solid and large, with a highly polished

brass knocker and letter-box and an electric bell-push adorning it. On the jamb to the right, two bell-pulls and the mouthpiece of a speaking-tube, all in brass and very bright. The lower bell bore a brass label: *Night Bell*. All were now mere ornaments and never used.

Littlejohn pressed the bell-push.

There were sounds of doors banging within and then of hurrying feet. An elderly woman in black appeared and looked enquiringly at him.

'Is Dr. Garnett at home?'

'Yes. This is his night off and there's no surgery. Is it urgent?'

The woman made no move to let Littlejohn enter. The training of years had given her a professional insight in dealing with callers and this one showed little anxiety or alarm.

'Will you please give the doctor my card and ask him if I may intrude for a little time?'

The woman glanced quickly at the card, relaxed and invited him indoors. She left him in a large dark hall, ornamented with many brasses and dominated by two large old prints, one on each side, of the *Charge of the Light Brigade* and *Napoleon's Retreat from Moscow*. The place was spotlessly clean and shining from effort.

The servant quickly reappeared and asked Littlejohn to follow her. She opened a door in one corner of the hall and led the way down a wide staircase to the rooms below.

The sloping site had given rise to a house with two storeys at the front and three at the back, the third being a basement facing the hills with its back to the road. They entered a room with a large window with a fine view upon open country. A door led outside and thence by a gently sloping path to a postern which gave on the road above through a wall which protected the grounds surrounding three sides of the building. This was the patients' entrance and the room Littlejohn and the woman had entered was the cheerful waiting-room. She tapped on another door to the right and led Littlejohn into the consulting room, beyond which was yet a further structure, a greenhouse in which, from the looks of it, orchids were being cultivated.

The doctor emerged and greeted him.

'Come in, Littlejohn...'

He washed his hands at a sink in the corner. He was medium built and portly with a ruddy round face. He resembled a retired admiral and was well-groomed and robust in his manner. He shook hands heartily.

'Take a seat. I was just spending half an hour with my plants. Are you interested in orchids?'

Littlejohn said that in a way, he was. He'd never cultivated them himself. His wife's father, Mr. Uprichard, had been a prominent grower in his day, however.

'You must come again and I'll show you my collection. Now, I suppose, you're here on business. Is it the Johnson case?'

'Yes, Doctor.'

'Take a seat. What would you like to drink?'

It was a pleasant room with another large window and a view of the distant hills now softened in the evening light. It was simply furnished: a large desk cluttered with the usual paraphernalia of instruments and papers, the doctor's chair and another for the patient, an examination couch and a spare armchair, instrument cabinets and a filing cabinet. A diploma of the Society of Apothecaries hanging framed over the fireplace.

'Whisky? Bring a fresh siphon, please, Mrs. Bull.'

The woman smiled and withdrew.

'My housekeeper. Been with me twenty years, since my wife died. I'm on my own. Two sons are doctors in practice, one in London, the other in Bristol. They don't fancy this place. What do you think of Plumpton Bois, Superintendent?'

Mrs. Bull brought in a silver tray with the whisky bottles, a soda siphon and two fine cut glasses on it. Littlejohn was glad when the drinks were ready and they could get down to business.

'Miss Johnson was your patient. Dr. Garnett?'

'Yes. And of my father before me. He and I have always attended the Johnsons. I was a surgeon in the Royal Navy until my father got too old to carry on here. Then I took over.'

'If any of my questions infringes professional confidence, please tell me, but I ask them to help with the case and for no other reason.'

'I understand.'

'You were, I believe, called-in when the murdered body of Savage was discovered.'

'That's true. He was, as you'll already know from the police surgeon's report, killed by a savage blow on the head with a poker, which, in simple language, fractured the skull and lacerated the brain. When I arrived on the scene, there he was, sprawled at the top of the cellar steps, quite dead. I saw him well within half an hour of his death.'

'No signs of any intruder then?'

'No. His wife, who's a hysterical creature, had kicked up such a hullabaloo that half the village had turned out. It was not only enough to scare off the murderer, but destroy all traces of him as well. Luckily our worthy P.C. Green was one of the first on the spot and kept the house more or less intact.'

'Miss Johnson had died within a month of this affair?'

'Yes. She had two strokes before the final one which killed her. She had been failing for some time. The last one put her in a coma and she slept quietly away.'

'No question of foul play there, then?'

Dr. Garnett seemed amused.

'I can assure you on that score, Littlejohn. No suggestion of foul play whatever. So the matter of one murder following another doesn't arise.'

'You were familiar with *Johnsons Place* and the family, doctor?'

'Yes. One can't say they were an unhealthy lot. Old Jabez Johnson, the one-time miner, who consolidated the family fortune and built the present house, died of strangulated hernia in 1920, at the age of seventy-five. Surgery wasn't as expert then as it is now and he got gangrene.'

Littlejohn raised his eyebrows and the doctor laughed. He was enjoying himself.

'You must think I'm a walking filing cabinet of all the cases my father and I ever dealt with. It isn't so spectacular as that. My father was a giant for records. He left ten volumes of closely written diaries as well as his ordinary medical notes. After the murder, I read up all I could find about the Johnson family. I'm a walking encyclopaedia of Johnson lore until I forget it all again. More whisky?'

He refilled Littlejohn's glass and took a good swig of his own.

'There are one or two points on which you can help us, then, Doctor, about the surviving family. How many children did old Jabez have?'

'His poor wife bore him eleven. Two were still born; two died in infancy, croup and meningitis. Two died of diphtheria before the age of twenty-one; and five, including Melody, two sisters and two brothers, lived on. There are records of the two sisters who married local men. One drowned herself and the other died in childbirth. When one reads such family histories, one realises, doesn't one, how short and precarious life must have been less than a century ago?'

'What happened to the sons, sir?'

'One was a harum-scarum, ran away from here and vanished from the records. Another left Plumpton as a young man and went to London. The murdered man, Savage, was presumably his grandson. That left Melody, who died in her bed at over eighty. I venture to say that had the whole of the eleven been the offspring of a contemporary Johnson, they'd all have survived with the help of modern medicine and surgery, until, at least, the follies of maturity had cut them down...'

'So, only the harum-scarum son remains unaccounted for?'

'Yes. And as he was older than Melody and would, were he still alive, be nearer ninety than eighty, we needn't consider him as a suspect, need we? One doesn't expect the senile to commit violent murder of the kind we're considering. Of course, Quincey Johnson – his name was Quincey, by the way, God knows why – Quincey might have had an offspring who did it. Though why they did, I couldn't even guess.'

'Sarah Rasp, sir...'

'Yes. As a Johnson family retainer, also a patient of my father and me. Record: bronchitis every winter and many years ago, a tumour of the breast successfully removed by surgery. She was also tested for spectacles by my father and both of us several times syringed her ears.'

'Was that all?'

'Should there be more?'

'This may be a bit near the bone of professional secrecy, doctor, but wasn't there an illegitimate child at *Johnsons Place* in your father's time?'

'By gad, Littlejohn, you fellows dig deep, don't you? You're right. There was a little bastard. Melody's child.'

'Do you care to tell me anything more about it?'

The doctor took another drink.

'I don't see why not. Miss Johnson is dead, the incident is old and forgotten, like the house she lived in. It was, of course, my father's case...'

The doctor pointed judicially at Littlejohn.

'By the way, tell me first whence you rooted out the information about Melody's child.'

'If you look through your front window, Doctor, you'll find the village stores almost opposite. On the night of the birth at *Johnsons Place*, the doctor's behaviour seems to have been under surveillance.'

'It still is. So you've been talking to Mother Murphy. One could write a book, too, about what goes on there at the front and the back doors. When Mrs. Murphy's four strapping daughters were at home, you'd have been surprised at the back-entrance traffic and who indulged in it. Yes, as I said, it was my father's case. He left quite a story about it in his diaries. Those diaries might have been called dynamite if time and the death of most of those concerned hadn't intervened. Jabez Johnson was alive at the time. He was an earthy kind of fellow but he wasn't having the family escutcheon blotted by a bar sinister. Neither was he going to allow his daughter's good name to be sullied or turn her out of doors melodramatically. He handled the matter with characteristic skill and thoroughness.'

The doctor paused to gather his thoughts.

'He kept his daughter out of the public eye at Plumpton Bois for three months before the event. Whether he found out the condition she was in or whether she told him, we'll never know. He sent Melody to Harrogate out of the way and then, probably just to confuse the trail if anyone grew suspicious, word got round, probably instigated by Jabez, that Sarah Rasp was pregnant. But it was Melody's baby my father delivered. Make no mistake about that. She returned home after dark shortly before the event. Why she didn't stay in Harrogate until it was all over is another puzzle. Old Johnson was an autocrat and doubtless dictated the programme. He must have wished to keep his eye on procedure because as soon as the child was able to travel, it was taken away.'

'Where?'

'I don't know. That's probably why Jabez insisted on the birth at *Johnsons Place*. He could see that his wishes and arrangements were fully carried out. My father even wasn't told where the child was going. Enough to say it wasn't smothered and buried in the garden. Johnson and Melody both said they would give information as to the child's whereabouts in case of need. I suppose it was adopted by somebody and brought up knowing nothing about its parents.'

'Who was the father? Do we know?'

'Not definitely. We can only surmise, as my father did. Several months before the child was born, Melody suffered a broken romance. She'd been engaged to David Hubbard, the local auctioneer, who, by the way, is still alive and living here. They were all set for being married, when suddenly Dave eloped with another girl and married her. Years later their marriage came apart and he returned here. Like his cheek after what he'd done, but that's Dave. Before he left Melody in the lurch, he must have seduced her and didn't know the result or even about the subsequent birth of the child. Otherwise, knowing Jabez Johnson, I'm sure there would have been a shotgun wedding if Dave had been around and hadn't complied willingly. But, by then, he was married and living elsewhere. That's all surmise, but it fits in with events. It also might explain why Melody agreed to dispose of the child. She probably couldn't bear to have Hubbard's brat about the place.'

'So, the child was taken away and vanished from local knowledge.'

'That's right. There is just one possible source of further information. Sarah Rasp. She was at *Johnsons Place* throughout the episode. She may know who took the child. I never followed it up. Why should I? Sarah Rasp left shortly after Melody's death. She's an old woman now. Gone to live with her sister, I hear.'

'Yes. We have her address.'

'Quick work! You'll be calling on her then. Let me know, just as a matter of interest, if you find any end to the story.'

'I will, sir. Meanwhile, was Miss Johnson a wealthy woman?'

'I don't really know. She was a careful woman and seemed to spend very little. For example, she was on my panel and not a private patient and, from what I've gathered during visits to the house, they lived somewhat frugally there. They made their own jams and did much of their own baking. At one time, the family were lavish. They were known for their liberal spending in the village in the way of tips and subscriptions. Jabez Johnson, of course, did it to show-off. He was that sort. Miss Melody, in days past, was good to charities and the church. Then, as though money had become more scarce with her, she grew parsimonious. That's what I heard in the village and there's not much that goes on there that I don't hear about. Finally, according to the probate notes in the *Povington Gazette*, she left a mere few hundreds and the house called *Johnsons Place*. Of course, that was nothing to judge by. She might have given or otherwise disposed of a lot of cash in her lifetime. Her banker or lawyer would be the best man to consult on that problem. And speaking of lawyers, Old Cunliffe, her solicitor, seems to have inherited all the loose money she left and the property passed to the unfortunate murdered man. Old Cunliffe was probably her only remaining friend from the old days. He did a lot for her during her lifetime and, as she had nobody else to leave it to, she passed her cash on that way. It's also well known that Cunliffe is very hot on the money and makes a habit of reminding clients when they make their wills that it's customary to leave what he calls a small memento to the lawyer. His wife is a very extravagant woman and he'll need every half-penny he can come by to make ends meet.'

The doctor rose and gathered up the glasses and replaced them on the tray. It seemed a hint that the interview was at an end.

'I don't think I can say much more that will be useful about the Johnson family. In estimating their wealth, I think one ought to remember that during the lead and zinc blende mining boom at Plumpton Bois, the place wasn't a Klondike. It was always known that there was lead here, but it wasn't exploited until around 1860. Jabez Johnson's father, known locally as Hoppity, it's said, bought the land at *Johnsons Place*, which was the name of his mine as well as the house he built, cheaply from a drunken crofter. Hoppity was a miner who'd been injured in the workings and limped badly, hence the nickname. Hoppity knew the direction of the lodes and guessed there was something good under the croft. His original mine shaft is in the garden at the back, filled-in now.

He ran a water turbine there from the stream which passes it. There were about a dozen mines going in the heyday, most of them small, with two large ones run by companies. Johnson's mine wasn't a bonanza, by any means. It was sufficient to raise Hoppity from the ranks of working miners to those of proprietors and enable him to live better than the average in the village. He must have saved a bit, too, for when the workings became too expensive to run profitably, Jabez, who followed in his father's footsteps, retired and lived comfortably, it seemed, on his savings. All the workings ran out about 1890 and Jabez lived about another thirty years after that.'

'You ought to write a history of the valley, sir.'

'It's all in my father's writings. There's quite a lot about the Johnsons there. When Hoppity had acquired his land, he hadn't the wherewithal to work it and had to borrow. He fought shy of banks and tried to obtain capital privately. My grandfather, Simon Peter Garnett, who was a mining engineer, attracted here by the local boom, lent him two hundred pounds, which was quickly repaid when the mine got established. My father knew of that and duly recorded it later. Somewhere in the Proceedings of the Povington Literary and Philosophical Society, there's a very good lecture on *Plumpton Bois and Its Mines*, which my father delivered. But this is merely small talk now, Littlejohn. It won't help you get your man.'

'But it is most interesting. You'd be surprised, doctor, how family background and history can help us sometimes in revealing motive and frequently the culprit in crime. I'm very grateful for your help.'

The doctor saw Littlejohn to the door and let him out. As he crossed the road to the inn, he saw the curtains of the bedroom above the village stores moving and could just make out in the dark background, the shadow of Mrs. Murphy.

9

SARAH RASP

It was raining hard at Frinton when Littlejohn arrived there. It looked high class even in the rain and there were a few visitors and men and women with dogs and swathed in raincoats wandering about on the seafront and in the shopping streets. The Superintendent had no time or inclination for the deserted beach and esplanade. He quickly found Jubilee Parade, a street with smart chromium-fronted shops at the sea end of it, gradually tapering off in the Colchester direction into a final quarter mile of seedy restaurants and snack-bars and toffee and souvenir shops.

'Second shop after the caff there,' said a scruffy lounger from whom he sought direction.

Mrs. Higgins' shop seemed a long way from the beach especially in the rain. The name was painted on the window. *Charlotte Higgins. Antiques. Junk* would have been a better description. The bulk of the stock was modern second-hand furniture with an odd piece of old pottery or bric-à-brac here and there looking forgotten and out of it in the confusion of jumble. The single large window was packed with the kind of stuff you find at the fag-end of a large auction sale and sold *en bloc* by the basketful after the crowd has tired and gone home.

Mrs. Higgins was sitting among it, wobbling to and fro in a rocking-chair, when Littlejohn entered to a jingle of bells over the door.

'Mrs. Higgins?'

'Yes.'

A dark, heavy elderly woman with a bit of a gipsy in her. Henna-dyed hair, dressed too young for her age with her skirt disclosing her fat calves, shrewd greedy eyes, and mean hands. The sort who would argue about the last halfpenny. She was smoking a cigarette stuck rakishly in one corner of her mouth and coughed a lot without removing it. She wore long ear-rings with red glass drops and a lot of jingling bangles and rings, as though she carried her whole stock of jewellery about on her person. She recognised Littlejohn as a policeman at once. She had an instinct that way. Her husband had served a term in gaol for receiving stolen gold medals on one occasion.

'Is your sister, Miss Rasp, at home?'

'What's your business with her? She's not been well and she mustn't be upset. Doctor's orders.'

'I won't upset her.'

He handed her his card.

'It's about the murder at *Johnsons Place*, where she used to live. I want some information and I think she might be able to help us.'

'I've heard that kind of tale before. Mr. So-and-so is helpin' the police with their enquiries. The next you see is that he's bein' hung for it.'

She left Littlejohn in the shop and shuffled in the room behind.

The place smelled of old neglected things; upholstery and dry rot, and the indescribable odour of cast-out household oddments which seem to pick up and preserve forever the aromas of stuffy bed- and living-rooms, shabby kitchens, sweating humanity and cats and mice.

She was soon back.

'You'd better come in the living-room. I don't want people to see the police carrying on enquiries in the shop. It gives the business a bad name.'

She jerked her head to make him follow her and led the way through a door with opaque glass panels into the place behind.

It was a sort of extension, an overspill from the shop, smelling just the same with shabby furniture parked all round the walls and a large table – probably once in a boarding house – with four cane-bottomed chairs at one end of it. A soiled cloth and a bottle of sauce on the table, a threadbare carpet on the floor, and Sarah Rasp sitting in another rocking-chair before the half-dead fire in the shabby old grate. She rose nervously as the pair of them entered.

'Here's the policeman who wants to see you. I told you you hadn't finished with them.'

Littlejohn told Miss Rasp he was sorry to disturb her and he thought she might be able to help the police on the Savage case.

Mrs. Higgins, by far the most pugnacious of the two, looked ready to stay on and intervene, but was suddenly interrupted by the arrival of a lorry with another load of old furniture, including Mr. Higgins himself. He stamped through the shop and presented himself. He was a small man with a bald head and a heavy moustache. He was wearing an old black suit with a morning-coat. He was like a dilapidated Crippen. He had been drinking and was truculent. The police had recently imposed a *No Waiting* ban right in front of the shop.

'Come on,' he said to his wife. 'We've got to get this lot shifted before the *cops* arrive.'

He underlined the word for Littlejohn's benefit and hustled his wife away, conveniently leaving Littlejohn and Sarah Rasp alone together.

They could hear Higgins bullying his wife. When he was in drink he was the boss, but when it evaporated he greatly feared Mrs. Higgins and frequently hid among the junk out of the way.

'I don't suppose you've made room for this new lot. You've been smokin' and rockin' again as per usual. Well, get crackin'...'

Miss Sarah Rasp seemed embarrassed.

'I'm only staying here tempor'y. I'm making arrangements for a flat of my own at the other end of the town where it's better class. She's only my step-sister and I'm paying for my keep here. It helps her, you see.'

Thus having divested herself of the indignity of her family and position, she asked him to be seated. He chose one of the cane-bottomed chairs, as the upholstered ones showed the shapes of the springs beneath their soiled covers.

She was a little shrimp of a woman, but she had a certain dignity. Her cheeks were red, probably from what remained of her healthy life at *Johnsons Place*, but wouldn't be so for long at this rate. She was civil and refined through contact with her late employer for so long. She was dressed in a black jumper and skirt by way of mourning for her dead mistress and her bright eyes and sharp upturned nose gave her the look of a friendly bird.

'I'm sure I can't help you with what you want. I'd gone when it all happened.'

'I hoped you might be able to give me an idea about the life at *Johnsons Place* when you were there, Miss Rasp. Some information that might help us.'

'I didn't even know the man who was killed. Miss Johnson never mentioned him, though I knew she had a great-nephew somewhere or other. I'm sorry about it.'

'Could I ask you one or two questions, Miss Rasp?'

'Yes, if you like, but I'm sure I can't help. Take your coat off. It's quite wet...'

She poked up the dim fire and hung the raincoat over the back of a chair to dry.

'How long were you employed by the Johnsons?'

'Over sixty years. I went to them when I was fifteen, and now I'm seventy-five.'

'You don't look that age...'

It was the usual compliment, but it seemed to please her. She smiled and nodded.

'Yes, I was one of the family. They took me from an orphanage and I stayed there for the rest of my life till Miss Melody died. My father and mother died when we were children. My mother married twice and Charlotte, Mrs. Higgins, was my step-father's child by his first wife. Her aunt took her to live with them; I was left to go to the orphanage.'

'Would you describe Miss Johnson as being well-to-do?'

Caught off her guard by that question, she gave him a frightened look.

'No. She had to be careful in her latter years. Her father left her enough to live comfortably on, I imagine. Of course, I never pried in her affairs. It wasn't my place. But she used to tell me now and then that we'd have to economise, as though having a struggle to make ends meet.'

'Why should that be? Do you know? You can tell me in confidence.'

'I understood from what she said sometimes, that investments had turned bad. She had lost money that way. She even said she had lost a lot of capital on English government investments. Not that I understood such matters, but she was very upset about it.'

'Did she go to the bank a lot?'

'At one time, she did. She used to go down to Povington every Friday to shop and draw her money. And then, as she got older, she stopped. She ordered the groceries and things by telephone and they came by the delivery vans.'

'How did she get the money to pay for things?'

'I don't really know...'

'Come, Miss Rasp. Even if you weren't supposed to ask about such things, you surely guessed.'

'She had a safe in the cellar. She always kept the cellar door locked. If anything was wanted down there or we wished to put things there for storage, she herself went down.'

'The safe was in a kind of closet cut in the rock behind the cellar wall, wasn't it?'

She clenched her fingers nervously.

'That's true. I knew about that because until the safe was put there I used to go down in the cellar freely. After it came she didn't like me going there. We used to call the little room in the cellar Mr. Johnson's glory-hole. He used to keep his papers and other private matters in it.'

'When did the safe arrive?'

'Six or seven years since. I can roughly remember it because it came while I was in hospital in Povington for an operation.'

'She kept a lot of cash in the safe?'

Sarah Rasp looked very uncomfortable, as though anxious to get away from the subject.

'I don't know, and that's the truth. As I said, she never got money from the bank after the safe came. I know, because she never went to the bank any more. Until then, the interest on her money used to arrive, too. Papers through the post which she took to the bank. That all stopped as well after she bought the safe.'

'She always carried the safe keys herself?'

'Never allowed them out of her possession. She slept with them under her pillow and they were there when she died. Even after her strokes, except the last two which killed her, when she couldn't properly walk, poor Miss Melody would go down the cellar almost crawling to get her weekly money from the glory-hole.'

'She didn't leave much loose money and the safe was empty when it was opened after the murder occurred. Can you think what happened to the rest of the money?'

Outside, Mr. and Mrs. Higgins were shunting the old furniture about from the lorry. They spent half the time quarrelling and abusing each other as she contended that Higgins was leaving all the weight to her. Added to this, there wasn't room for it in the shop and she was insisting on his taking some of the old stuff from the shop to a warehouse they had somewhere or other. Their conflicting voices rose and fell and punctuated the interview in the room behind.

Sarah Rasp was very uneasy. She sensed that Littlejohn knew more than he was telling her and he felt the same about her.

'Did anybody go down to the safe after Miss Melody died? If you know, you'd better tell me. Miss Rasp, as we have means of finding out from other sources.'

'I don't know, and that's the truth. I wasn't there all the time. There was the undertaker to see to and the funeral. I couldn't be in half-a-dozen places at once or be watching all that everybody did.'

'Who had the keys after Miss Johnson died?'

'I took them from under her pillow for safety and then I gave them to Mr. Cunliffe, the lawyer, as soon as he arrived. She died at four in the early hours and he was on the doorstep by ten o'clock the same morning. But I never went down the cellar. What sort of woman do you think I am; the mistress not yet cold and me robbing her safe? It's not fair of you.'

She began to sob.

'Don't take on so, Miss Rasp. We don't suspect you of anything. Did you tell Mr. Cunliffe about the glory-hole and the safe?'

'No. I forgot with all the trouble and he didn't ask me about anything. He didn't want anything from me. I was only a servant, as far as he was concerned, to be seen and not heard.'

Knowing Cunliffe, Littlejohn could understand that very well.

'Miss Johnson didn't leave you anything in her will, did she?'

'No.'

'After more than sixty years' service. Wasn't that strange?'

The woman was very troubled about something.

'I'd better tell you, sir, if you'll regard this as between the two of us...'

Littlejohn nodded agreement, knowing more or less what was coming.

'She was good to me while she was alive. I won't have a wrong word said about Miss Melody.'

'I'm sure you won't. How was she good to you?'

'She paid me well.'

'In more than wages, too?'

The reply came suddenly, as though she wished to get it said before she changed her mind.

'Yes, she did. After her first stroke, she said I'd always been good to her and loyal and she gave me a present of cash. And another after her second stroke. Why shouldn't she? It was her own money and she'd nobody to leave it to. Except that Savage chap, who cared only for what he could get out of her.'

'Don't worry, Miss Rasp. I'll keep this to myself. I'm merely concerned with who killed Mr. Savage, not with private matters between you and Miss Savage during her lifetime.'

The woman seemed greatly relieved.

'I'll tell you this, sir. If she hadn't given me those presents, I'd have had to find other work after she died. I'd not saved much and I couldn't live on my old-age pension... At least, not the way I was used to living at *Johnsons Place*. It made me feel a bit independent and I shan't have to live here when my welcome's at an end. I'll be much obliged by your not mentioning it to anybody else. Mr. Cunliffe was suggesting that I might have had money gifts from Miss Melody, but I told him a lie. I said I hadn't. He'd have made me give them back. I know he would. You see, she left him what remained after the house. I must admit that he'd been good to her and looked after her affairs.'

'We'll forget money matters then. There's another point I want to ask you. Was there a child born at *Johnsons Place* many years ago?'

'Who told you that?'

She had turned ashen and looked ready to faint.

'Don't worry about it, Miss Rasp. Nothing wrong. I just want details about it. You can help us.'

Sarah Rasp sighed heavily. This was indeed her bad day.

'It was an awful thing and best forgotten.'

'The child was Miss Melody Johnson's?'

'Yes...'

She paused still embarrassed and not knowing what to say about it.

'It doesn't seem fair to the dead to be talking like this about her.'

'Don't forget, Miss Rasp, that this isn't idle gossip. It may help us to find who killed Mr. Savage.'

'I don't see that it has anything whatsoever to do with the murderer, if you don't mind me saying so.'

'Who was the father of the child? Do you know?'

'No. Not for certain. You don't talk about those things outside the family. Or, at least, you *didn't*. Nowadays it's different; you boast about it to all and sundry...'

'Isn't it true that Miss Johnson was shortly to be married when it occurred. And that Mr. Hubbard, her fiancé, eloped with and married somebody else?'

'Yes. He mustn't have known she was in that certain condition when he left her in the lurch. And when Miss Melody told her father, Mr. Hubbard was already married, and much good the other woman did for him.'

'All this seems to have been kept very secret. They didn't even know in the village?'

'No. Why should they? They didn't shout such things from the housetops in those days. Mr. Johnson, who worshipped Miss Melody, seeing she was all he'd got left of the family, took it very bad at first. He was like a madman, threatening to kill Mr. Hubbard, and such like. But he was very kind to Miss Melody about it, arranging everything. When the child came, those who suspected anything thought it was me as was in the family way and not Miss Melody. They couldn't have believed it of her, that's certain. I didn't tell them otherwise. Not that there was much they could complain about. Half the children in the village was either born on the wrong side of the blanket or well on the way before their parents were married.'

She smiled as though proud of her share in tricking them.

'The child was adopted by someone?'

'He was put in a Christian orphanage and later adopted.'

'By whom?'

'Mr. Johnson insisted on having it all his own way. The rules of the orphanage were that the child never knew his real parents and those who adopted him never knew either. It was all to the good and made it that there shouldn't be any trouble later, such as real parents claiming him back et cetera. I must say that Mr. Johnson was sorry later. He wished they'd kept the child. It was all done impulsively, as you might say, to keep up the good name of the family and Miss Melody.'

'The name of the orphanage, Miss Rasp? Do you know it?'

'It was a place called Saint Margaret's at Helsham, in Sussex. A nurse came for the baby one night and took him there. Miss Melody found it hard to let him go, but her father wouldn't agree to anything else. As I said, he was sorry later. I remember the name of the orphanage very well, because it was the place where I was brought up before I went to *Johnsons Place*. Mr. Johnson used to subscribe to it even before they got me.'

'Strange they should have parted so easily with the child, especially as the pair of them were all alone, and all that remained of the family.'

'Mr. Johnson, as I said before, was old-fashioned and regarded it as a shame on the family, especially as it happened in the way it did. I mean, Mr. Hubbard betraying Miss Melody and then eloping with somebody else. I think Mr. Johnson felt he couldn't hold up his head in the village as things were. He was that sort. A proud man and all the more so because his family had risen from nothing. He was firm about it, although he never, in my hearing, reproached Miss Melody. Later, when they'd got over it, they did try to find out about the child, but the rules of the institution were against it and they persuaded Mr. Johnson that it was for the best. And quite right, too. Once a baby's been adopted, you can't have people quarrelling about who shall have it.'

'So the child might be anywhere now?'

'That's right. It's terrible to think of. It was an awful thing that Mr. Hubbard should do such a trick and them unable to do anything about it. The child was best out of the way of gossip and in the hands of good parents.'

She suddenly seemed to awake to something.

'We keep saying "the child this and that". If he's alive, he must be almost an old man now. I wonder where he got to?'

It sounded like an old-time melodrama and probably the passing of time had made it more so.

'There's nothing more you might think would interest me, Miss Rasp?'

She hesitated.

'There was something else that passed through my head as we were talking... Oh, yes. It was about Miss Melody's brother, Ben Quincey Johnson. Did you know she had a brother? I never knew him. He'd gone before I arrived.'

'Yes. A kind of prodigal son, wasn't he, only he didn't return home?'

'That's it. Benjamin was always a difficult boy and he got with a bad lot in Plumpton. Drinking and generally acting like hooligans. He left home and was never seen again. The police came to see his father and complained that if he wanted to keep Ben out of prison, he'd better get him to mend his ways. Mr. Johnson gave Ben a good hiding. Ben was eighteen at the time, but his father was a big strong man. Ben took it bad and left home. Miss Melody and his father tried later to trace where he was but they never found out and he never wrote. She even advertised in the papers for him.'

'How long since she last advertised? Was it in the local papers?'

'Several years since. It was in the London papers. I remember her writing the advert and sending it by post. Then she stopped. I think he must have written to her, although I never saw any letter. And he must have changed his name, too.'

'Why do you think he wrote?'

'I think she sent him some money. I once came on her putting a lot of pound notes in an envelope. A funny thing, too, it wasn't one of those registered ones. Just an ordinary one, but it was a lot of money she put in.'

'Did you see the address?'

She hesitated and coughed behind her hand.

'Well... You see it was so unusual and it made me curious. I didn't mention this to you before. It seemed a bit mean what I did. But now, as there's been a murder I'd better tell you, sir. It might be important. She'd written the address in ink and as I came in the room, she slipped the envelope in her desk and locked the drawer. When she left, I put the blotting paper in front of the mirror. I could just make out the words *Mr. J. H. Walker, c/o G.P.O. London*. I felt sure he'd changed his name and it was really Mister Ben. Who else could it be? She never went out those days and had no contacts, as far as I know, with anyone of that name. He was always in trouble and that kind of man often has to change his name so he can't be traced.'

'Any district number after *London*?'

'No. It was all mixed up with other writing and, in any case, I don't remember it if there was any number.'

Littlejohn made a note of it.

'How long ago would that be?'

'Four or five years... I can't be sure.'

'Did you ever see any more letters like that?'

'No. She must have taken it to post herself. I never saw another one. Perhaps he'd written and told her he was still alive and needed money. I don't know how much she sent him. And then, perhaps, he never wrote again. It seemed he didn't want her to know where he was living, him giving a post office address like that.'

Four or five years ago! Like hunting for a needle in a haystack.

'And that was all?'

'Yes.'

'Well, thank you for your help, Miss Rasp. If you do happen to think of anything else, will you let me know? You can either write a letter or send a postcard and ask me to call on you again.'

'I'll do that, sir.'

Outside, in the shop, the Higgins pair were still tumbling furniture about. He kept swearing at her and bullying her. Finally, Mrs. Higgins appeared at the door, red faced and dishevelled.

'Haven't you two done yet? All this talk and me left to lift the stuff about the shop because my husband can't stand properly and see straight. It's not fair...'

She stood there, determined to put an end to her sister's idling.

Littlejohn rose and put on his raincoat. He thanked Sarah Rasp again for her help, gave her his card, and then threaded his way through the litter on the shop floor.

It was still raining. Higgins himself, like a drowned rat, was unsteadily cranking-up his old lorry. He offered Littlejohn a lift. Higgins ought really to have been booked for driving alcoholically, but Littlejohn just thanked him for the offer and declined. He felt he had enough on his mind. First Frinton; now Helsham. He wondered how many more outlandish spots the case was going to lead him to before it was all settled.

10

AT THE BANK

The large, solid edifice of the Home Counties Bank stood in the best position in the main square of Povington. A Georgian building, it had been erected by Messrs. Vere, Pett, Boumphrey and Company, later changed to the Bank of Povington and then absorbed in the massive body of the London bank. It was shortly to be altered extensively and changed to a very modern horror of concrete and glass.

When Mr. Parkinson, manager of the branch, learned that his betters proposed to pull down the old building and erect a new one around him, he at once informed Head Office that he would like to retire on pension as soon as possible as his health would not stand the transition. He was due to go at the end of the year.

When Littlejohn entered the bank the head porter hurried to him and asked what he could do for him. This official who, in the good old days had been clad in a maroon uniform with gold trimmings and wore a top hat, was now dressed rather like a postman, much to his disgust. He took Littlejohn's card and bore it off down a carpeted corridor to the manager's office, leaving Littlejohn to watch the busy six cashiers transacting business at the long heavy counter under the watchful eyes of Vere, Petts and

Boumphreys whose portraits were to be removed to the local art gallery when the new building was begun.

Mr. Parkinson, who was smoking a cigarette and reading *The Times*, threw back his head and read the card on his desk through his half-moon spectacles.

'Oh, hell! Better let Mr. Routledge see him.'

'Mr. Routledge is out, sir, taking his cup of tea.'

Mr. Parkinson scowled.

'He's always out. All right, Ellams. Bring the Superintendent in. Another forgery or more information about how to avoid bank raids, I suppose. Put out the sherry.'

The messenger softly padded to a cupboard in the wall and took out a decanter with a badly hidden gesture of disgust. He was president of the local Band of Hope and handled the vessel as though it might have been a bomb. Over the marble mantelpiece, laden with a huge marble clock, the portrait of the last Mr. Humphrey Pett-Boumphrey looked down in disgust. He had been Mr. Parkinson's grandfather and with the departure of his grand-son, the last of the old line would vanish from the bank.

Mr. Parkinson was a tall heavy man with a bald head shaped like a coconut, florid features, heavy jowls and a Roman nose. He wore a smart black jacket, striped grey trousers and spotless white linen and a rimless monocle dangled on a cord round his thick neck. He regarded as unprofessional the free-and-easy style of dress assumed by his colleagues and staff and only a reproof from his directors had prevented his insisting on their dressing like a lot of tailor's dummies. He rose to meet his visitor, having first fortified himself by taking snuff from a huge silver box on his desk, a century-old relic presented to the late Arthur Vere Pett to mark his fifty years as treasurer of the Povington Infirmary and Lunatic Hospital.

The messenger presented Littlejohn. Mr. Parkinson was surprised. He'd expected a man in uniform whom he could put in his place, for he was a J.P. Instead, here was someone as well-turned-out, but more comfortably, as Mr. Parkinson himself. He at once bade him take a seat and offered him a glass of sherry, which he called sack in memory of his forebears who had drunk from the same bottle and glasses since the foundation of the bank.

'You're a stranger here, Superintendent ah... Superintendent...'

'Littlejohn...'

'... ah... Littlejohn. What can I do for you? You here on police business or privately? I see you're from Scotland Yard.'

'Yes, sir. I'm investigating the crime at *Johnsons Place* in Plumpton Bois.'

Mr. Parkinson looked hard at Littlejohn over his half-moons.

'I don't see how the bank is affected by that. Do you?'

'You will remember Miss Melody Johnson, no doubt. I believe she kept her account here.'

'Of course I do. But the murder wasn't connected with her, was it? I gathered the victim was a bank clerk related to her. Am I right?'

'That is so.'

'Then you've come to the wrong bank, Superintendent... ah... Superintendent...'

'Littlejohn, sir.'

'... Littlejohn.'

'I don't think so, sir. It's about Miss Johnson that I'm here.'

Mr. Parkinson rummaged in the snuff box again, took a pinch, threw half of it on the floor, and inhaled the rest. Then he dusted himself down.

He generally went through this pantomime when about to say No to importunate customers.

The room was utterly quiet. Double glazed windows, padded door, high ornamental ceiling, graceful furniture. It had the atmosphere of a private chapel.

'I wonder if you could tell me something about Miss Johnson's finances before she died.'

'Not much. She didn't keep an account of any size with us.'

His tone gave the impression that most of the accounts in his bank were massive and impeccably conducted.

'Yes; but once it was quite considerable, wasn't it?'

Mr. Parkinson raised his thin sandy eyebrows in surprise. Had some of his staff been betraying confidence?

'You seem to know quite a lot already, Superintendent.'

'Miss Johnson's papers are still at her lawyer's. We've had access to some of them.'

'I see. Well, I can tell you in confidence, that she was very comfortably off at one time. No doubt she still was at her death, but we were in no position to judge. She took most of her money away from this bank. *And*, I believe, she didn't take it to a competitor, but held it all in cash at home. It arose through her crass stupidity in money matters and her refusal to take the advice of those who knew better than she did.'

The memory of it all caused Mr. Parkinson to grow flushed and petulant.

'I didn't deal with her myself; my deputy, Compston, used to look after her affairs. He's since been promoted to London, but we keep a comprehensive system of records here which I read as they are compiled. I know most of what goes on...'

As though it weren't his job and he had merely kept a benevolent eye on things!

He pressed one of the keys on an office telephone near his desk.

'Yes, sir.'

'Bring me the file of the late Miss Melody Johnson, please.'

'Yes, sir.'

A pause and then a tap on the door.

'Come in...'

A young lady under a beehive-shaped mass of fair hair and with oval black spectacles appeared with a file of papers and placed them on the desk.

'Thank you, Miss... ah... Miss...'

'Nankivell.'

'Ah... Nankivell...'

The door closed behind her.

Littlejohn wondered if Mr. Parkinson knew his own name. He seemed quite unaware of anyone else's.

Dead silence, punctuated by the rustling of the file as Mr. Parkinson perused it, his half-moons focused from the end of his nose.

'Ah, yes. It comes back to me now. Miss Johnson inherited around thirty thousand pounds from her father, who kept a good account here in his time. The legacy was in cash and good securities. That was in 1920.'

Amazing! Forty-five years ago! Littlejohn wondered how far back the dossiers extended.

'Matters proceeded quite normally until about six or seven years ago. The investments had their ups and downs. There were railway stocks which suffered sadly and others which increased in value. From time to time. Miss Johnson invested more money in this or sold that investment, always taking our advice, I see. Then she had a slight stroke which is mentioned here...'

The bank seemed to keep the health records of customers, too, apparently!

'... It must have made her a bit queer in the head. Old age, I suppose. We never know how it will be with ourselves, do we?'

Mr. Parkinson sighed, polished his glasses and took some more snuff.

'By the way. Do you take snuff, Superintendent er...?'

'No thank you, sir. I'll smoke my pipe, if I may.'

'By all means, please do. Where was I? It says in the file that she informed us she wished to sell £20,000 of War Loan, bought at around 101, which at the time of the record here, was quoted at 60, and would realise about £12,000, leaving her with a capital loss of £8,000. It seems she didn't understand the stock markets properly and said she thought if she invested in government stocks she'd get her money back intact when she wanted it...'

Mr. Parkinson's eyes became filmed with confusion and he bumbled about in the file petulantly.

'Dear me. Compston must have been away on holidays or something. The minutes are very confused here...'

Finally, he seemed to see the light and closed the file as though the very sight of it made him feel sick.

'The shock of the information seems to have affected her brain. She sold *all* her investments then. When the proceeds arrived here for credit of her account, she withdrew most of the money in cash and took it away with her, leaving an odd hundred or so in case she needed to issue any cheques. It remained there until her death.'

Mr. Parkinson leaned back confidently in his chair now, as though again in complete mastery of all the facts.

'By that time Compston had obviously returned, for the records become more coherent and intelligently compiled. I gathered that he at once got in touch with Mr. Cunliffe, Miss Johnson's solicitor, informed him what had been going on, asked for an explanation and begged Mr. Cunliffe to co-operate with the bank in putting matters on a more reasonable basis. Have you met Mr. Cunliffe, senior, Superintendent... ah...?'

'Yes, sir.'

'How did you find him?'

'Difficult.'

'Exactly. He was difficult about the matter we are discussing. Compston, it appears, explained to him about all the cash which Miss Johnson was proposing to keep at home in that lonely house with only another woman living there with her. A decidedly dangerous position. Compston also told him that, after mature consideration he had, himself, written to Miss Johnson a letter, which she could calmly peruse and think over, advising her not to keep so much cash at home, but to return it to the bank for safe keeping, and if not re-invested, then in her account. Do you know what Cunliffe replied?'

'I can guess.'

'You are right. He curtly told Compston to mind his own business and not to bother Miss Johnson any further. He, Cunliffe, would take full charge of the matter and be responsible. Well... Cunliffe has a good account here and so has his firm. We didn't wish to antagonise him, much as it went against the grain. The matter was discreetly dropped.'

'I see, sir.'

'I'm glad. I gather from the will, which I have perused, that Mr. Cunliffe, senior, inherits the balance in the account of Miss Johnson here. He hasn't withdrawn it yet, but I'm sure he will do so any day.'

The look he gave Littlejohn and the testy way he said it implied that to remember a cantankerous lawyer and to forget her banker when she made her will was just too bad.

'How much cash did she withdraw, sir?'

'Thirty thousand pounds. Strange she should finish up after all those years, with their ups and downs and gains and losses, with roughly what she started with.'

'And that was about six or seven years ago?'

'Yes. In 1959.'

'Did she mention to you or your deputy her need for a safe?'

Mr. Parkinson tapped the file approvingly.

'It is mentioned here. Before she even drew out the cash she asked Compston if he could recommend a good safe maker. He gave her the name of our friends Stubb's. She got a safe from them.'

'What is their address, sir?'

'You wish to check what I have told you?'

'I want to enquire about the routine of getting the safe to *Johnsons Place*.'

'I see.'

He pressed another key of his talking-box.

'What is the London address of Stubbs', the safe people?'

Without hesitation the box spoke back.

'Sixty-four, bee, Moorgate, E.C.2.'

'Thank you.'

Littlejohn made a note of it.

'You think, sir, she put all that cash away in the safe?'

'I'm sure she did. You see, the Bank of England notes changed in style after she took the cash away from us. She must have heard or read about it and feared the old ones wouldn't be valid any longer. She brought in all the old ones on three separate trips and changed 'em for the new issue. It caused quite a commotion at the counter. I have a note in the file in the then chief cashier's own hand, recording the transactions.'

'Thirty thousand in cash is a large amount, sir. Especially to keep in a safe in one's home.'

Mr. Parkinson made an irritated gesture.

'I quite agree, Superintendent... er... I quite agree. But, as far as we were concerned we handled it perfectly regularly. She asked for cash and she had enough in her account at the time. Also she resisted our advice and Cunliffe was somewhat vociferously watching her interests.'

Mr. Parkinson grimaced again.

'You ought to see Cunliffe.'

He grinned sardonically, displaying two even rows of teeth, certainly false ones.

'He'll give you a warm reception, I can assure you...'

The case seemed to have its roots in the past when the characters now involved might have been more easy-going and approachable. Melody Johnson, Cunliffe, Mr. Parkinson, old Doctor Garnett, Hubbard... Now, those who remained were old, proud of success and position, cantankerous and contemptuous.

Cunliffe certainly ought to be the next on the list for interview. He knew more about Melody Johnson and *Johnsons*

Place than anybody else. But he was a self-opinionated lawyer, difficult to question, if he allowed himself to be questioned at all, and hostile when he thought it to his advantage.

The problem would have to be faced, however, and a way found to make Cunliffe talk. Otherwise the enquiry might drag on indefinitely for lack of the information he was withholding. Already, it seemed, the case had become divided between two camps; the local Chief Constable, who supported Littlejohn in the belief that the murder of Savage had its roots in something which had happened in the past of the Johnsons; and the local police supported by Cunliffe, who thought the crime purely fortuitous, arising from a casual robber and only to be resolved by casting a wide net and capturing the culprit that way.

'I shall have to do my best with Mr. Cunliffe, sir.'

'I wish you the best of luck, but I don't envy you.'

There seemed to be little more to discuss with Mr. Parkinson, who didn't appear to take an intelligent interest in the police work, although anxious to be patient and polite about it.

Littlejohn rose and thanked him for his help. This appeared to please Mr. Parkinson who always liked a little appreciation. He sat pondering on how he could assist further. Then something suddenly seemed to strike him.

'You were interested in the safe. Could I help you further with that? What did you wish to know about it from Stubbs'? They are shortly due to install a new strongroom and a number of new safes in these premises and are in a good mood with us.'

'One of my colleagues will probably call on them in London and find out exactly what happened when Miss Johnson's safe was delivered.'

'Plummer, the man who supplied it, is still with them, I know. Would you like to speak with him from here over the telephone? It might save you a lot of time.'

'That's very good of you, sir.'

Mr. Parkinson took up the instrument and quickly brought Stubbs' to the line.

'Give me Mr. Plummer, please...'

He was there, recently promoted from sales representative to high executive office. He shouted so loud in what was supposed to be delighted greeting that Littlejohn heard every word he said.

Mr. Parkinson somewhat laboriously explained why he wished to speak to him.

'Yes, yes, Mr.... er... He's with me now. I'll put him through to you.'

He handed over the phone and after a few brief greetings Littlejohn and Plummer got down to business.

'You remember supplying the safe Mr. Parkinson has just mentioned to you. Did you visit *Johnsons Place* and see Miss Johnson?'

'Yes, I did. She asked our advice about a safe to be kept in the cellar, burglar and fire proof, for purposes of holding cash and valuables. She wanted a second-hand one but we had none available. We recommended a suitable model and she bought it. I examined the cellar because naturally with such a heavy and cumbersome object one needs to survey the landscape beforehand, so to speak. There was a primitive sort of strongroom there. A queer cavelike place built by Miss Johnson's father, she said. He'd actually excavated it in the solid rock. It was just the thing. That was all. All went well. No trouble.'

'How many keys were there?'

'Two. A single lock with duplicate keys. I believe she kept one herself and the other was held by her lawyer. I also recollect her ordering a third key. She wrote to say she required another in case she lost or mislaid the one in her possession. We had the number and particulars and supplied a duplicate key. It was sent to her by registered post. That is the usual way where personal delivery isn't made. I asked her if I should deliver the key myself, but she said I needn't come so far; the post would do. It was quite safe to do it that way. She acknowledged the key, paid our bill, and that was the end of the matter.'

Littlejohn thanked him and then he thanked Mr. Parkinson again.

'Any help?'

'Not obvious help, sir, but the information may be very useful later.'

He bade Mr. Parkinson good-bye and left him.

Outside the sun was shining. There was an open-air market in the square and stalls had been put up around the periphery; vegetables, drapery, dairy produce... A cheapjack offered to sell Littlejohn a watch at a price that would surprise him. The clock in the little tower over the corn exchange struck half past twelve.

'Better get it over,' said Littlejohn to himself and made his way through the crowds in the direction of Cunliffe's office. He found the bank messenger waiting on the steps.

'Excuse me, sir. Mr. Parkinson said I'd probably find you on your way to Mr. Cunliffe's chambers. There's a telephone call come to the bank for you from an Inspector Cromwell, sir. Would you please return and take it?'

'It's very civil of you... Yes, I'll come.'

Cromwell and Littlejohn had earlier parted company in Plumpton Bois; Littlejohn off to Povington and Cromwell to canvas the village and then call at St. Margaret's Orphanage at Helsham for as much information as he could get. Littlejohn had told him where he might find him if anything important cropped up.

Mr. Parkinson had taken the call in his private lair, still called the Board Room by the staff, and was sitting smiling at the instrument which lay on his desk, as though he and the man at the other end were old friends and he was keeping him company whilst he waited.

'Here he comes,' he said to Cromwell. 'Good-bye... Don't mention it, Inspector er...'

'Hullo, Cromwell. I was just on my way to Mr. Cunliffe's office.'

'Good job I caught you before you got there, sir. I've something to tell you. Something important. Perhaps I'd better not mention it over the telephone...'

'I'll defer my visit until after lunch, then. I'll return to Plumpton and join you for lunch at the *Miners Arms*. I'll wait for you.'

'Pity you need to return, Superintendent... er...' said Mr. Parkinson as Littlejohn laid the telephone down. 'We might have had lunch together.'

After a starchy beginning, Mr. Parkinson seemed to have taken a fancy to Littlejohn.

11

ST. MARGARETS

C romwell left Plumpton in a borrowed police car at seven o'clock on his way to St. Margaret's Orphanage at Helsham. He rubbed his hands together as he crossed the rough courtyard at the back of the inn. It was a bright sunny morning and he proposed to breakfast on the way.

Littlejohn was still in bed. He was due to make a round of local calls mainly in Povington to see Miss Johnson's former bank manager, and it was no use starting before the place was warmed up.

Cromwell reached his destination at ten o'clock after a comfortable run at high speed. He liked fast driving, although his wife and family continually rebuked him for it and kept him in order when they accompanied him on week-end jaunts. The orphanage was easily found for it dominated the village and was its sole claim to fame, except the beauty of its position. A vast Victorian edifice with long wings built on behind, situated in parkland with large old trees dotted about it and formal flower beds decorating the lawn in front of the Gothic façade.

There was a school there, too, situated in a big separate pavilion not far from the main buildings and as Cromwell drove down the main drive, he could hear a percussion and recorder band beating out a country dance. He stood on the steps listening with approval until the music ceased and then he rang the door-bell. As he waited for an answer, the band struck up again.

There was no reply to the bell, as though the band drowned all music within earshot but its own. So he turned the knob and entered.

Absolute silence indoors, except for the distant sound of recorders, drums and tambourines. He found himself in a large square hall lighted by a great dome-like window over the broad staircase which lay ahead of him. There were framed pictures, obviously painted by youngsters, hanging almost on top of one another on all the visible walls, as though some kind of exhibition were in progress. Cromwell, the father of three daughters, felt irritated that duty prevented him from doing the rounds of the show.

There wasn't a soul about. There was not even a smell of cooking, which would have been appropriate in a place of that kind at that hour. He began to think he had got in the wrong shop.

Then he saw a room to the left, labelled *Superintendent*. It made him feel more at home and he knocked briskly on it.

'Come in.'

A large, lofty room with broad bay-windows overlooking the front lawns and geraniums, and a long table crammed with books and papers from end to end. A multitude of small chairs arranged around it, as though the board of management gathered there for their meetings. There were crowded bookshelves from floor to ceiling on three sides of the room and a fire burning in the old-fashioned hearth, although the day was mild out of doors.

In a space cleared among the litter on the table, a man in a grey flannel suit and a woman in nurse's uniform were examining lengths of flowered material. They had obviously been disturbed in some earnest task; both stood, almost like pillars of salt, staring expectantly at the intruder.

The man was middle-aged, lightly built, with ruffled grey hair, gold-framed spectacles and a small grey moustache.

Cromwell, who had a mnemonic scheme of his own for remembering people, by which he identified strangers by linking them with familiar portraits in the rogues' gallery of Records Department, thought he rather resembled William Herbert Wallace, suspected of murdering his wife in 1931 in Liverpool, but who got off on appeal.

The woman was small, too, middle-aged, buxom and fair and she seemed to be thoroughly enjoying herself. Both of them gazed benevolently at Cromwell.

'May I speak to the Superintendent, please?'

'You are already doing so,' fluted Mr. Wallace, who then said he was called Wooller and at the same time introduced Miss Popple, the matron.

Cromwell handed him his card.

'Dear me! What have we done wrong?'

Why did they always say that? But Mr. Wooller didn't seem in the least perturbed. His conscience was obviously clear. So was Wallace's when he was arrested, but that didn't matter for the time being. Matron, on the other hand, flushed deeply, as though she had something to hide.

'You're the very man, Inspector. Which of these four patterns do you think the most tasteful?' asked the Superintendent in his high-pitched voice. Matron gave him a smiling look as though she adored him.

Cromwell must have looked astonished. He was wondering if he'd got the right place or stumbled in a mental home by mistake. The pictures in the hall might have been...

'I believe in the principle of one thing at a time, Inspector. Matron and I have been arguing for half an hour about material for new curtains in the staff common room. Once we settle that problem we can give your enquiries, whatever they may be, our more concentrated attention.'

'Now!'

Mr. Wooller spread the four samples on the table.

Flowers in profusion, spring and autumn leaves, birds resembling purple parrots perched on brown branches, and a complicated system of entwined hops suitable for decorating high-class beer-glasses.

Cromwell chose the parrots without really knowing why he did so, but in a bewildered effort to get to his own business.

Matron gave a squeak of delight.

'You see, Superintendent. He agrees with me!'

She looked ready to hug Cromwell.

Mr. Wooller, it seemed, had chosen the hops, but he yielded with a good grace and told Miss Popple to get on with the order before the board of management changed the patterns again. She gathered up the samples eagerly, bade Cromwell a cordial goodbye, and he didn't see her again.

'And now. What does Scotland Yard require with St. Margaret's?'

Mr. Wooller had a shrill resounding voice for his size, but Cromwell, regretting somewhat his thoughts about W. H. Wallace, found him very pleasant and accommodating. If he treated the orphans he superintended as well as he treated Cromwell, they ought to be a happy lot.

'It's an enquiry about an illegitimate child you admitted many years ago, sir.'

Mr. Wooller looked very grave and sorry and made fending-off gestures with his hands.

'I must tell you, Inspector, that such matters are very confidential. When children are brought to us in such unfortunate circumstances, and especially if they are later adopted, it would not do to supply information to the public which might embarrass the child or its foster parents. It would not be fair. It is like the confessional, you know. Sacred, in a manner of speaking.'

Mr. Wooller smiled sternly and looked almost ready to bow Cromwell out. And then he had second thoughts.

'If it happened years ago, perhaps we might consider it. It all depends on the nature of your questions. Tell me about it.'

Cromwell did.

Mr. Wooller looked a bit relieved but still a bit bothered.

'Born around 1904! Good heavens, the child must be sixty now! Older than myself. Whatever do you want with him? He may be dead by now.'

'As I said, sir, his mother, a Miss Melody Johnson of Plumpton Bois, seems to have been a liberal subscriber to your home. I don't suppose there will be a record of who was the father, but if not we must content ourselves by finding out the name and address of the foster parents. We wish to know if the man is still alive and where he may be at present.'

'I will get the records. They are kept in the muniments room. Please excuse me. I may be away for a few minutes.'

'In that case, I'd like to take a look around the exhibition of children's pictures in the hall.'

Mr. Wooller was puzzled.

'Children's pictures? Good gracious!'

He giggled.

'Those are the works of the late Theodore Varnish. He was said by some people to be the modern Douanier Rousseau. He left an annual income to our institution on condition that the works you saw – also bequeathed to us – should be exhibited for three months of every year. If, like the Douanier, Varnish acquires posthumous fame, we may have inherited a large fortune.'

Mr. Wooller looked very doubtful about it all and although Cromwell didn't know what he was talking about, he nodded knowingly. The pictures had lost all interest to him, so he sat by the fire until Mr. Wooller returned.

The Superintendent was carrying a huge, leather-bound register and a small file of papers and panting from his efforts.

'There!'

He flung his burden among the shambles on the board table.

'I am sorry I can't invite you to help yourself, Inspector. The contents of this book and the files are strictly private and even to allow them out of my hands would greatly displease the board. We might, however, go together through the points which interest you. What, in particular, do you wish to know?'

'Is the child – or man, as he now is – still alive?'

Strange, how even after so long, the cause of all the commotion sixty years ago was still pictured as an infant in swaddling clothes!

Mr. Wooller polished his spectacles and licked his lips.

'That, I must say, is an investigation more up your street than mine. We don't as a rule, pursue our inmates when they leave us, especially when they are mere babies. Our duty is to ascertain if would-be foster-parents are worthy and capable of bringing up the child in the way he or she should go. It would not do for us to become glorified probation officers watching over every child that leaves our hands.'

'Can you give me the name of the foster-parents of the boy and where they came from?'

Mr. Wooller thumbed over the pages of the huge register, like a clergyman about to read from holy writ. He found the page he was seeking and his lips moved as he read the entries.

'Ah!' he said reverently to Cromwell. 'You would be surprised at some of the names in this book. Some have become members of parliament... or even higher than that...'

Cromwell wondered if some of them had even become kings, or princes, or even film stars!

'But to business. The adoption papers were duly executed and are in this file...'

He pointed to the cardboard folder on the table beside the book.

'... The mother, Miss Johnson, signed the agreement to the

procedure and her father, Jabez Johnson, countersigned it. As this all happened sixty years ago and the information is to help the law, I can't see that divulging the names of the foster-parents can do any harm. They were Arthur and Sarah Agnes Mellish, of this parish. The child was adopted by a Helsham couple and christened John Henry.'

'Was anything further seen of them or the child after adoption?'

'Fortunately, yes. The Superintendent here at the time, 1904, was a Mr. Augustus Gladman, M.A. He was a copious diarist and even went so far as to annotate the minutes of the board of governors and the register of inmates with light comments and gossip in his own handwriting.'

Mr. Wooller's tone implied that he practised no such levities.

'I see he made a few entries here after adoption. In 1904, his note by the side of the foster-parents reads "Very worthy people. Well known to me... Mellish is the village carpenter. He built my greenhouse." I notice the official entry describes Mellish as builder and undertaker, but I don't suppose that matters now.'

Cromwell sighed. Between them, Mr. Gladman and Mr. Wooller were going to take up a lot of his time.

'What was their address, sir?'

'Oh, they're both dead. You won't find them there now. They've built a garage where their old cottage stood.'

'But there will be relatives.'

'Yes. As a matter of fact, one of the Mellishes is a gardener here.'

'Could we talk with him and ask him what happened to John Henry?'

'He's a very talkative man and once you get him going, he'll waste a lot of time...'

Yet another artist, along with Gladman and Wooller, in circumlocution. All the same, it was in the course of duty.

'In any case, there's no need. There's a note here on the

register that John Henry Mellish joined the army in 1939. Such notes, it seems, were made, where possible, for purposes of our War Memorial. Mellish isn't marked as a casualty, but he never seems to have returned to the village. We and his remaining relatives are described as completely losing trace of him.'

'Doesn't the gardener Mellish know?'

'No. We made extensive enquiries when our War Memorial was compiled. Nobody, including Sam Mellish, the gardener, seemed to know what had happened to him.'

'Were the War Office asked?'

'I couldn't say. I wasn't here at the time. Doubtless enquiries were made there about Mellish, along with those of the rest.'

Mr. Wooller seemed exasperated that his categorical statements should be in the least doubted. He closed the register.

'One moment, sir. What was Mellish's regiment?'

Mr. Wooller, laboriously and with facial movements which seemed to indicate that he was praying for patience, consulted the record again.

'The second Loamshires.'

'Thank you, sir.'

'Anything further, Inspector?'

'The file on the table, sir. Does it contain more of Mellish's records?'

'Yes. And some items of correspondence referring to him in the past.'

'May I ask the nature of the letters?'

'Really, Mr. Cromwell. *All* this is certainly irregular. If I seem to have waived the rules, it is to help the law. But...'

'Remember, Mr. Wooller, this is a case of brutal murder.'

'Dear me! I'd forgotten. It is not up to me to impede the course of justice, but I fail to see whatever in the world a man like John Henry Mellish and his records can have to do with your case. I must do my duty as I see it, however. What was your question?'

'The letters in the file. What are they about? If you don't mind.'

'They concern enquiries, like your own, about Mellish's whereabouts.'

'By whom?'

'By Miss Melody Johnson. About five years ago, she wrote to us asking the very questions you have asked yourself. She wished to trace him. Not that she intended claiming him as her son, but simply that she wished in making her will, to include him as a beneficiary. I was here then and was obliged to reply that we didn't know where he was, as I have done to you.'

'And there the matter ended?'

'Well, the correspondence did. But we then had a visit from her lawyer. A Mr.... Let me see. I made a minute of my report on the incident to the board.'

He rummaged in the file.

'The lawyer was a man called Cunliffe. A very rude and domineering man. He accused me of being unhelpful and said my letter was peremptory. What else could I say I wrote quite politely, for Miss Johnson was a good subscriber to this institution. I wasn't able to tell the man anything more, except to give him the name of the regiment. He went away without a word of thanks and I was glad to see the last of him.'

'And thus the matter ended.'

'I'm afraid so.'

'Thank you very much, sir. May I use your telephone, please? I would like enquiries to be made about Mellish at the War Office.'

'Of course. Use the instrument on my desk.'

Cromwell rang up Scotland Yard and asked that the requisite enquiries be made about Mellish and the result telephoned to him at Plumpton.

Then he thanked Mr. Wooller again and bade him good-bye.

On the way out he met a gardener, sitting behind a hedge, setting out his lunch on the grass. Hunks of bread, cold sausages, and an onion.

'Morning,' he said through the open window of the car and stopped.

'Mornin'.'

A small, knotted, wiry man with large hands and blue eyes.

'Is your name Mellish?'

'No. Mine's Behag. Sam Mellish just left for his dinner. He lives in the village and goes home on his bike. If you was wantin' him, you'll ketch him along the road.'

Morning school was over and the children were trooping across to one of the annexes behind the house. Mr. Wooller, who had been watching Cromwell's departure from the window, now appeared at the front door shading his eyes with his hand like the father of the prodigal son, and wondering what Cromwell was up to with Behag. Surely not discussing the identity and history of Johnson's orphan with him!

Cromwell turned out into the road. In the far distance he could see a solitary cyclist in the middle of the avenue slowly pedalling along and apparently in no hurry for his food. He accelerated and drew alongside the cyclist. A long, lean, hop-pole of a man, whose wife looked to have cut his hair with scissors and a basin. His face was shrivelled like a walnut, and he had close-set washed-out blue eyes. The aged bike he was riding was a bit small for him and was shorn of all non-essentials. He had to pedal in bow-legged fashion to keep his knees free of the handlebars.

'Mr. Mellish?'

Cromwell stopped and Mellish dismounted with some difficulty.

'That's me. I just seen you at the orphanage talkin' with old Wooller as I was mowing the lawns.'

Cromwell passed out his cigarettes. Mellish took one and lit it, almost setting fire to his straggling moustache.

'Did you know John Henry Mellish?'

'You mean Artie Mellish's adopted boy. Artie was a second cousin of mine. There's a lot of us Mellishes in Helsham. Artie had four children, two boys and two girls, not countin' John Henry. They've all left the parish.'

'But I thought they adopted John Henry because they couldn't have any children of their own.'

'They did. But the good Lord changed His mind after they got John Henry. Two years after they took over Jack, as he was called for short, four offspring was born to 'em, one after another. Jack was left out of it, then. A pity. It did him no good. He was a bit of a wrong 'un, was Jack.'

'What happened to him?'

'If that's what you've been seekin' at the orphanage, old Wooller was no help, I'll bet. Thirsty sort of day, isn't it?'

Cromwell passed him two half crowns to put him in a talkative mood, although Mellish seemed to be enjoying himself as it was. A passing car hooted at them for monopolising the road and they drew in to the side.

'Sorry, I can't take you to the village pub for a drink, Mr. Mellish. I'm a bit pushed for time. But you can get yourself one when I'm gone.'

The money vanished somewhere in Mellish's disreputable old suit and he thanked Cromwell heartily.

'Jack was a bad lad. His father used to beat him, but it did no good. Always playin' truant, never at school, pinchin' folk's apples and pears, then, when he got older, runnin' after the girls. He was a good lookin' chap. Put a local girl in the family way and ran off instead of marryin' her. The child died at birth, which was as well for all concerned. One Jack in the village was enough. Then, just before the war, he turned up again with a wife who might have been a tinker's daughter and he did-up an old empty cottage and they lived there like pigs. No children, for some funny reason or another. Some said they wasn't married...'

The record of John Henry's misdeeds looked like going on for ever.

'How did he end-up?'

'Left the woman in the lurch and joined the army. He'd been livin' before that on what he could scratch together. Odd jobs, poachin', and, as likely as not, other things that wasn't as straight. At any rate, he was too crafty to get himself in trouble with the police. Then, when he joined-up, he called on Artie and his wife to say good-bye. Artie was quite touched by the thanks Jack gave him and how he sort of apologised for the way he'd behaved in the past. When he'd gone, Artie found he took with him eighty pounds his missus had saved and kept in a drawer in the dresser. But what upset Artie more than the money was that Jack had also taken his gold watch that Colonel Longland at the Grange had given him after his fifty years' service as a bellringer at the church, the colonel being the leader of the team. All the same, Artie didn't tell the police. He said he wouldn't have the Mellish name dragged through the courts. So Jack got away with it. That was the last they saw of him.'

'Was he killed in the war?'

'Yes. But not officially. Most of the lads here joined the Southshires, but one of them, Seth Clark, was himself in the Loamshires. He'd joined because it was his father's old regiment. He came upon Jack Mellish there. But Jack, perhaps because he thought the police would be after him for what he'd done at home, had 'listed in the name of Walker. Jack pretended not to know Seth, which didn't break Seth's heart, for the less he saw of him the better he was pleased. He said that Jack was always in trouble. Jack and a pal of his, a chap younger than himself but just as bad, was always in hot-water of some kind or another. Then Jack was killed in the D-Day landings. Seth said he saw him shot down dead on the beaches. Jack's pal came through, but Seth never saw him again.'

'I see. Is Jack's name on the village War Memorial?'

'It is not. Neither is it on the orphanage one which is in the hall at the house at present covered by them awful pictures somebody left them in his will. Rubbish, I call 'em. Kid's paintin's... You see, there never was a Walker in the village, nor in the orphanage by the looks of things, so John Henry was lost touch with and nobody bothered.'

'And that was the end of that.'

'Yes. The woman he left behind quit the village quick enough. Artie and his wife died and the family was scattered... An' I'll get scattered, too, when I get home and my old woman's been waitin' with my dinner... So, I'll wish you good-day.'

He swung his leg over his bike and adjusted himself to the pedals and then wobbled off on his leisurely way home.

Cromwell called at the village to telephone Littlejohn and then made off as fast as he could go.

12

DAVE HUBBARD

L unch was almost over at the *Miners Arms* when Cromwell arrived back from Helsham to report to Littlejohn. They finished their meal under Crabb's ill-disguised displeasure, for he liked to close the dining-room and count and put away the takings before half past two. It left him plenty of time to take his ease and drink a lot of whisky before dinner-time. It was late in the afternoon before the two detectives ended comparing notes and discussing their further steps in the case.

Littlejohn had deferred interviewing Cunliffe and had decided in view of Cromwell's news of the lawyer's interest in the Johnson child at St. Margaret's, to leave over a visit to Cunliffe until next day.

Meanwhile, Cromwell had certain matters to attend to at Scotland Yard in connection with a prosecution for forgery. It was arranged that he should leave for London right away in the borrowed police-car, stay overnight, and then return to Plumpton Bois after a call at the Elephant and Castle branch of the London and Southern Bank, where Savage had worked and where the manager might be able to add to the background of the murdered man.

After seeing Cromwell off, Littlejohn rang up the home of David Hubbard, the estate agent and auctioneer, to whom, years ago, Melody Johnson had been engaged. Hubbard, it seemed, was expected back about five o'clock and Littlejohn found him already there when he called.

Hubbard's house, *Belle Vue*, had been built by the owner of the largest mine in the palmy days of Plumpton Bois. A large, square stone residence standing back from the road on top of a bank which had been excavated to hold a large double garage. There was a paddock behind in which a roan mare was grazing, for Hubbard, in spite of his age, did a bit of riding now and then for the benefit of his liver. There were fine views of the hills and countryside from the terrace in front of the house.

Hubbard's housekeeper, a voluminous, pleasant country-woman, opened the door and at once invited Littlejohn in. As soon as he crossed the threshold he found himself in an atmosphere of warm and fastidious comfort. The hall was lighted by a large window at the turn of the fine staircase and another in the roof above the stairhead. It was furnished in obviously care-fully chosen and valuable antique pieces with pictures by Wilson Steer and Walter Sickert on the walls. The room into which the woman led him was even more attractive. Large and light, with a window overlooking open country at each end; it was not over-crowded but such furniture as it contained was choice Georgian of the best period. Persian carpets on the floor and a discreet selection of water colours and prints on the walls. Copley Field-ing, David Cox. Rowlandson... There was a portrait of a racehorse by George Stubbs over the fireplace. The cabinets full of costly china...

It was obvious that Hubbard in his capacity as auctioneer had personally skimmed some of the cream off sales in the once opulent houses of the locality. He was sitting among it all, at his ease, taking tea. There was an aroma of toasted scones hanging about. He invited Littlejohn to join him.

Hubbard was a small, thin man who might, in his earlier days, perhaps have passed for a jockey. He was dressed in a light tweed suit, but riding habit would have suited him better.

Littlejohn had learned that he was eighty or more, but he carried his age well, his small dark eyes were bright and interested in what was going on, his lined features aquiline and healthy. There was nothing of the cattle dealer about him. He had obviously been a part of the wealthy landed community of Plumpton Bois district and had assimilated their culture and ways whatever his beginnings might have been.

'I thought you'd be calling sooner or later, Littlejohn. Come and join me at tea and we can talk in comfort.'

His face twitched now and then with the nervous tic Littlejohn had noticed when they first met.

The housekeeper had already produced another cup and saucer and Hubbard poured tea for the Superintendent and handed out the scones. They passed from trivialities to the case in hand.

'This seems to be a confused case, Superintendent. Some say it is a random sort of crime, committed by a wandering intruder seeking what he could get and then suddenly alarmed by the unexpected arrival of the victim. I hear that that is the view of the county police except the Chief Constable. Others, including the Chief Constable, think that the crime has deeper roots than that, hence your arrival here, as an independent expert to handle the affair. So, I assume you hold the same view as the Chief, or else you wouldn't be remaining here, as the local police could deal with a tramp or casual burglar who murdered Savage...'

He was lolling deep in his armchair, quite relaxed. He might have been talking about crops or cricket.

'You're right, sir. I do believe there's more in this case than meets the eye. The roots of the crime seem to go deep into the past and although I've no proof whatever that an investigation on these lines will be successful, I've a hunch I'm on the right track.'

'So, you're getting close to knowing who murdered Savage?'

'No, sir. I've no idea whatever. We haven't yet got to that part of the investigation. We're gathering information. The police here are still busy on the case which bears out their theory and are combing the area for newcomers, strangers, no-goods who might have been in the vicinity. In one sense, they've relieved me and my colleague of a lot of routine work. We've had the time to get to know much of the Johnson background, but there are still gaps in our knowledge. When we've filled them, we shall, I'm sure, be very near a solution of the case.'

'Have you called on me for a general discussion of the affair, Superintendent, or to ask me questions?'

'Questions, sir. You've lived in this district all your life. You know it better than anyone hereabouts. You can also, I know, tell me a lot of the past history of the Johnson clan. Some of it will, no doubt, be painful to you. I hope you'll excuse any questions which fall upon raw places. I assure you it's not impertinent curiosity which prompts them, but purely to keep up with the case.'

Hubbard gave him a wry grin.

'Ask away. I assure you that as far as I'm concerned, the past is dead, the wounds are gone and I've grown a carapace that will resist all efforts to hurt me. You'll be merely digging up dry bones which leave me cold and which will probably do you no good, either. However, fire away.'

'I gather, sir, that you were once engaged to be married to Miss Melody Johnson.'

'By God! That's a good first shot! You've been hard at work on the past, haven't you? Who told you that?'

'If you'll answer the questions, sir, I'll tell you all the sources when we reach the end. You were engaged to Miss Johnson, and the marriage didn't take place. May I ask why?'

'Because she found out at the last minute, that she didn't love me. That was the reason.'

He even laughed. A hard, sarcastic sort of cackle, as though he were cynically dealing with a long past drama in the life of a third party which amused him. Littlejohn realised that in his contacts with these old people, these relics of events of more than half a century ago, he was among those in whom the fires of passion and enthusiasm were extinguished forever. Many of the characters had quitted the stage long since. Their shadows were all that remained for those left behind to hate or despise.

'She loved someone else.'

Littlejohn said it quietly and there was no reply, as though the answer was obvious.

'She was pregnant at the time she broke-off your engagement. And the child was not yours?'

'Your industry amazes me, Littlejohn. Do you know, you have stumbled on a secret that was only known to very few. To Melody herself, of course, to her father, Sarah Rasp, and the doctor... and, naturally to the people who arranged the adoption of the child. Old Johnson saw to it that not another soul knew of it. I was only let into the secret because I argued about the matter when she told me she didn't love me. I thought it was just a woman's whim, at first. Nerves. She soon convinced me.'

'The father of the child. He must have known.'

'Why *must*. At any rate, he didn't marry her, did he? He either wasn't told, or else he wasn't in a position to marry her. He was a married man already. Otherwise old Jabey Johnson would have made a shotgun affair of the wedding. He was that sort.'

'You left the district for a time, I heard.'

'That is true. I was terribly shaken, because I loved Melody in those days. I couldn't believe it when she told me. She wasn't that kind. I just packed a bag and went away. I got married very soon after that. I suppose I felt the need of some comfort. It was either that or whisky. I'm sorry I didn't choose whisky. I assume you know all about it.'

'Yes.'

'I didn't marry a second time. Had enough for one lifetime. But who in hell told you all this bygone history?'

He paused.

'There's only one source. It's Cunliffe himself. How did you get him to spill the beans?'

'You say Cunliffe himself, sir. What's the significance of *himself*. Was he involved in it?'

'I don't know any more than you do.'

'But you think Cunliffe might have been the father of the child?'

Hubbard suddenly sat bolt upright, his eyes large and round.

'Your source of information certainly wasn't Cunliffe! He'd never have told you that. You must have been quizzing Sarah Rasp.'

'She wasn't my informant either.'

'Then you've arrived at it by a process of deduction on the information you've gathered. As in my case. Nobody told me. I don't believe Melody told a soul. Not even her father, who'd have exploded and gone for the man like a mad dog, married or not. You are not to take my word for it. I only know that when he was a young man, Cunliffe was a bit of a rake. He married early in life, a fairly wealthy girl rather on the plain side, but of a prominent family in the district. He soon tired of her and sought his pleasure elsewhere. There was no question of divorce. She was a Catholic, though Cunliffe wasn't. Cunliffe wasn't anything...'

Hubbard rose, crossed to a cabinet and took out a decanter of whisky and a siphon.

'You'll take a drink with me, I hope. Our talk has now reached channels where tea isn't appropriate...'

He poured out a stiff drink for each of them and splashed soda in them.

'Where were we? Cunliffe. One day at the club in Povington, a fellow member, later killed in the first war, was chatting with me when Cunliffe entered the bar. My friend was half drunk and talkative and after he'd made a few unpleasant comments about Cunliffe, said to me "You want to keep an eye on Cunliffe and your girl..." Before he could say more, I told him that would be enough or I'd knock him down. But it made me think. I'd no suspicions at all, but you know what an effect a whisper of that kind can have on a man's morale when he's in love with a woman. I found out that what the chap had said was true...'

He spoke slowly with a touch of malice in his tone.

Littlejohn had a feeling that never before had Hubbard talked to anyone so frankly of the tragedy of the past. Through all the years since the man he suspected had ruined his happiness, Hubbard had nursed his secret until the right time came and he could reveal it and destroy him.

'You've met Cunliffe? You wouldn't think such a cantankerous old bag of bones would have been worth a second look from a lovely and... to use an old-fashioned word that's now laughed at... virtuous girl like Melody Johnson. But he was good-looking and energetic in those days and as self-confident and impudent as he is now in his old age...'

Hubbard might not have been past eighty himself. He only saw the wreck his rival had become.

'... I found that what was said in his cups by my friend was true. Cunliffe had taken a firm fancy to Melody. At the club dance and the hunt ball his attentions were embarrassing and talked about, to say the least of it. He was in deadly earnest...'

Hubbard nodded his head to emphasise it and took another drink from his glass.

'... And he has been ever since.'

'Ever since? You mean...?'

'I mean that if he'd been able, he'd have taken her from me and married her, instead of wrecking all our lives. Melody seemed to be rushed off her feet by it. She was happier for it, though God knows why she should have been. I spoke to her about it, but she shrugged it off and said it was me she would soon be marrying, wasn't it? In the end I went to see Cunliffe in his office and told him to keep away from Melody. He was, as usual, impertinent about it. "You're going to marry a damned pretty girl. You ought to be flattered when other men admire your choice." You can see, Littlejohn, that I'm not a big chap and in those days, Cunliffe almost made two of me. But I'd a hunting crop in my hand at the time and belted him over the head with it and knocked him down. And I left him where he lay. Nothing more was said about the incident and for a time, Cunliffe kept away from Melody. Then she sent for me shortly before the wedding and called the whole thing off. You seem to know the rest. When I refused to believe her and insisted on going through with it, she told me about her condition. I accused Cunliffe, but she denied it so emphatically, that I was tempted to believe her. I was still willing to marry her, child and all... She said she'd never marry.'

He shrugged his shoulders as though he cared no more for the past, but his eyes were hard and his lips tight.

'To satisfy my own morbid curiosity I later made some enquiries about the movements of Cunliffe over recent months. Melody had been on a holiday to Malvern with a friend that summer. I found out that Cunliffe had been absent at the same time. I went to Malvern and made more investigations. He'd been there. That seemed to explain everything. The information was no use to me. I'd found the solution to the mystery. I let it rest. Now it's all come out because a little pip-squeak inherited *Johnsons Place* and couldn't wait to search it for the cash his aunt might have left behind. How is what I've told you going to solve your case?'

'It will help me to make Cunliffe talk.'

'You are not to say you obtained it from me.'

'I won't. I promise you that. After all, you say it's only your deductions and you were never sure.'

Hubbard nodded.

'Right.'

'You mentioned Cunliffe's being deadly serious, then and now, about Melody Johnson. What do you mean?'

'Since he seduced Melody, he's never looked at another woman. That must be fine and dandy for Mrs. Cunliffe. He and Melody even remained friends. She might have been his mistress, for anything I know. I wouldn't be surprised. He remained her lawyer...'

Hubbard cackled harshly again at the irony of it.

'Yes; her lawyer. After her father's death, he more or less took charge of her and her affairs. The rake reformed had become a model of propriety. He had no children of his own and I'm sure would have taken Melody's baby under his wing. But old Jabez Johnson was alive and saw to it that the whole affair was hushed-up and the child disposed of and with far-away foster-parents. I'm certain Jabez never knew who the father was. He'd have killed Cunliffe. He was a man of violent temper and tremendously strong. He died about 1920 when it was too late for Melody or Cunliffe to undo what had been done about the baby. Had Mrs. Cunliffe died, Cunliffe might have married Melody. But she didn't. She's still alive. She carries her years better than her husband and if she did know anything of his affair with Melody, it must delight her to have outlived her.'

'You have been very frank, sir.'

Hubbard gave Littlejohn a senile, peevish look.

'You needn't think I'm taking this opportunity to turn over a lot of idle gossip or nonsense from the past. And I'm not unburdening myself of it all out of self-pity or to make you sorry for me. I was as bad as Cunliffe was. We were a rotten lot round here in those days. Life was easy and money easily come-by for some of us. Even when I got engaged to Melody, I'd another string to my bow; the woman I married after Melody threw me over. She ran away from me with a parson. I'd have forgiven her anything. Even a chimney-sweep. But a parson...'

He had drunk three stiff whiskies to lubricate his tale and was now running away with himself.

'I was saying, wasn't I...? I was saying that I wasn't seeking your approval of my conduct in those days. I'm telling you because I'm sure that Savage fellow came upon some secret or other as he was rifling *Johnsons Place* or else he encountered the murderer also in search of something. I don't know what it was. Was it money? Or papers? Or a diary or records which would bring trouble on someone? My theory is that the someone was Cunliffe. He was there to find whatever incriminated him before the new owner of the house brought it to light. And they met. Now, all's fair in love and war. But this is murder...'

Littlejohn rose to go.

'Have another drink, Littlejohn. Don't go. I want to know what happened to Melody Johnson's child. Have you found out?'

'He's dead. He was killed in France in the last war.'

'So you did get to know about him. Tell me some more. What kind of man did he turn out to be?'

'Not very good. Unfortunately, the foster-parents who adopted him thinking they'd never have any children, followed the adoption by producing several of their own. It must have had a bad effect psychologically on the adopted one. He became difficult, almost delinquent. Then he joined the army at the outbreak of the last war, got into trouble several times there, but atoned for it all by getting killed during the D-Day landings in Normandy...'

'He had no children?'

'Not that we know. He fathered a child, which died, on a local girl but didn't marry her. He was living with another woman in an old cottage in Helsham until he joined the army.'

'Following in father's footsteps as regards the women, eh?'

'I don't know. We don't really know very much about him.'

Littlejohn rose again.

'Well, Littlejohn, I hope I've been able to tell you something which'll help you in your investigation. But remember, not a word about where the information came from. I've no wish to appear in court on a slander charge at my time of life. I'd have great difficulty in substantiating some of the statements I've made to you. Everybody's dead who could have supported me. And Cunliffe's a vindictive man...'

Littlejohn pitied Hubbard, too. On his own in the world, surrounded by good taste and comfort, and yet still nursing hatred and revenge against the only man alive who belonged to the dead days of his past.

13

ARMY RECORDS

The London and Southern Bank had only just opened its doors before Cromwell arrived in the rain in the colourful neighbourhood of Elephant and Castle. The branch was a new one in the New Kent Road. Mr. E. Arthur Butt, the manager, was busy in his room engaged in his opening task of solving the *Daily Cry* crossword puzzle, when Cromwell arrived. Mr. Butt commuted daily by train with a number of friends who competed with each other in a joint effort to master the enigma as far as they could on the journey and, before they met again on the return home, an endeavour to fill in the blanks.

Mr. Butt looked very worried as he greeted Cromwell.

'Perhaps you can help me, Inspector, before we get down to business. This sounds in your line. A clue in the *Daily Cry* crossword. "Big biceps to make arsenic sandwiches". Any idea? Word of nine letters...'

'Armstrong,' said Cromwell without hesitation.

'Done it! You're a marvel. But why Armstrong?'

Cromwell told him. The Armstrong case was still a classic one. Thus supplied with a vital clue, Mr. Butt in a few strokes finished his task in triumph, rang for some coffee, and settled down to work with his visitor. He explained to Cromwell that business didn't warm up until mid-morning and that meanwhile it was his custom to relax a little after his long journey from Billericay.

Cromwell told him the purpose of his visit.

'Savage. A great pity. He was due to retire in the course of a couple of years...'

Mr. Butt's face lengthened and he bowed his head momentarily, as though paying a passing tribute to his deceased colleague.

'We have missed him, although he was a bit of a difficult man to have about an office. One shouldn't speak ill of the dead though...'

Mr. Butt took his coffee in little sips, offered Cromwell a cigarette and lit it for him.

'Difficult, did you say, Mr. Butt?'

Mr. Butt shrugged his shoulders as though he wasn't really making a serious complaint.

'He just had a chip on his shoulder, that's all. You see, he came, I believe, on his mother's side, from a wealthy mining family, but his father had quarrelled with the members of it who held the money. Savage had tried to effect a reconciliation, but had been snubbed. He hadn't got on very well in the bank. He ended up as second cashier on the counter here. It wasn't that he hadn't ability. No; that wasn't his main trouble. He'd a rash and impulsive temper and was subject to little fits of rage in which he said and did things which were later held against him. To hold high office in a bank, one must be patient and discreet. Savage, by his indiscretions, offended customers and what is more where promotion is concerned, he offended the high officials of the bank. That is all over now, I'm sorry to say, and I won't bore you with examples.'

'This business of his family quarrels...'

'Savage hadn't done the quarrelling. He tried hard to make it up with his aunt. I think that he hoped by a substantial legacy, if he could ingratiate himself with her, he would achieve a certain amount of independence from the bank and give himself the prestige he hadn't been able to acquire in his work.'

'Did he talk freely about his expectations and disappointments?'

'Yes, when he was complaining about what he regarded as unjust treatment in the way of promotion or increases in salary. He would boast of his family and their wealth and how, when he came into his patrimony, he'd leave the bank at once. Then, he would have one of his fits of depression and confide his troubles to one of his colleagues. A man of strange moods. I was never in his confidence, but I got to know most of what went on. A manager usually does from one source or another.'

'Did you know about his eventual benefit under his great-aunt's will?'

'Yes. He came to see me about it. He'd heard from her lawyer that he'd been left her house in... where was it...?'

'Plumpton Bois.'

'That's it. Plumpton Bois. He really wanted the day off to go and see the property, which he said was a very desirable one, judging from what he'd heard of it from his people. It seems that was all that came his way. No money. He was furious. As a matter of fact, he talked right away of contesting the will on the grounds of his aunt's senility. He said he was the only member of the family left and, at least, a fair share of the money ought to devolve upon him by right. I told him not to be rash. In his usual fashion, he was going to rush into it like a bull at a gate. I told him to go and see the lawyer, ascertain the circumstances, and then think about it, before committing himself to extravagant legal expenses which he might find himself eventually having to pay.'

'A very wise bit of advice.'

'He took my advice, but he said he was going to write to the lawyer at once, mention the fact that he knew his aunt was wealthy, and ask what had happened to her fortune. I told him he would be far better in waiting until he could discuss it with the solicitor face to face, but I knew he didn't agree. He wrote his letter and received a dusty answer. The lawyer told him that Miss Johnson was quite of sound mind when she made her will and that how she disposed of the rest of her estate was her own business and her own choice and that Savage could think himself fortunate, after taking no interest in his aunt for so long, to receive any legacy at all. Savage came and told me about it.

'In his letter to the lawyer, he'd suggested calling to see him on a date about a week from the time of writing. The lawyer had agreed. Now, Savage was determined to go as soon as possible. He asked for the day off following the receipt of the lawyer's reply.'

'Did he warn the lawyer that he was going?'

'No. As usual, his reaction to the affair was cock-eyed. He said he wasn't going to forewarn the solicitor of his intended visit, after all. He was proposing to descend upon him unexpectedly. In his usual paranoid fashion of thinking, everybody was against him and plotting to do him out of his rights. He said the lawyer... I think the name was Cunliffe... was up to something. That there was legal jiggery-pokery afoot. I warned him again not to be silly, but he'd made up his mind. He took the day off. And you know the result. He found himself in a hornets' nest and lost his life. Not that I'm suggesting for a moment that Cunliffe murdered him. Don't get me wrong. But I am suggesting that had Savage bided his time and gone there on the date originally arranged, he wouldn't have found the intruder there and things would probably have turned out all right. After all, he could have sold the house for quite a nice little sum, if what Savage said about it was true. And all this tragedy and trouble wouldn't have occurred.'

'My chief, Superintendent Littlejohn, met Mrs. Savage, but didn't find her very helpful. She was disappointed in the house and could never have considered living there. The Superintendent visited her in hospital where she'd been receiving treatment for shock.'

Mr. Butt helped himself rather absent-mindedly to the

remnants of the coffee in the pot. It was cold, but he didn't seem to notice it. Outside the road had grown busier and busier, the traffic hummed past and although the frequent lorries on their way to and from the docks were not to be seen, their enormous loads were visible, sailing past above the ground-glass screens of the windows, like goods on a conveyer belt.

'I can't say that I care much for Mrs. Savage. She was a temporary clerk in our bank during the war and that's how Savage met her. To tell the truth, the bank was glad when Savage took her off our hands. She wasn't much good in an office. The sort who thought she was doing the bank a favour working for us at all. I'm sure a lot of Savage's unhappy moods and irritable behaviour were due to her. She was always pushing him and doubtless either urged him to be continually asking for promotion which he didn't merit, or else upbraided him because he wasn't getting on as fast and well as she wished. When I read in the paper that she was in a state of collapse, I thought how like her to make an exhibition of herself and put on an act. Poor Savage. He didn't have much luck.'

'Had he any enemies or anybody who didn't wish him well, sir?'

'You mean, did any of his colleagues or customers follow him down to Plumpton Bois and kill him? The very idea is ridiculous.'

'It's a question I must ask, Mr. Butt. Savage, to put it rather unpleasantly, seemed always to be upsetting someone or taking the wrong line of conduct in matters. Could he possibly have involved himself in some serious quarrel with anyone?'

'Not that I know of. You can talk with the staff if you like. But I'm sure if Savage had been in serious trouble anywhere, I'd have got to know of it. I flatter myself I'm an approachable sort of manager and have the confidence of my staff.'

'I won't go into that matter further then. Was he a steady sort of man? No betting or excessive drinking? No ways in which he might have become personally involved in unpleasantness?'

'You mean owing money he couldn't repay, say to bookies or

for gambling debts. The very thought of it makes me laugh. Savage in the hands of bookmakers or moneylenders, or even surreptitiously keeping another woman! Good Lord! He was a model of correct behaviour. I think you know that a bank keeps a strict eye on that kind of life. We *have* to do so. You can take it from me that Savage led a virtuous and impeccable life in that respect. His wife, I know, was an extravagant woman and made a habit of keeping up with the Joneses, if you know what I mean. But Savage knew how to look after his money. He was well insured and I'll tell you in confidence, he kept a nice balance in his account at this office. He wasn't involved in money troubles at all. And, as for women. I cannot imagine Savage as a Don Juan. I think he'd had quite enough of the opposite sex in his experience with Florence, his wife. I'd go so far as to say that I think he despised women. He was a bit naïve in that respect and thought they were all like his own wife.'

Cromwell smiled grimly.

'It's often that kind that come a cropper when they get the chance. However, we won't press that point. Did Savage serve in the forces during the war?'

'Yes; there again, he ended up as a second lieutenant instead of a brigadier, as he thought he should. He was in the Pay Corps. Will there be anything more, Inspector? I have a client due at eleven.'

'No, thanks, sir. It's been obvious all along that Savage wasn't killed for any personal motive, but we just had to check. Your information and help have been of great use and I'm grateful for your co-operation...'

Outside the rain had ceased and it was warm and pleasant. Cromwell felt he'd earned a bit of fresh air and set out to walk back to Scotland Yard across Waterloo Bridge. Cromwell loved London. He stood for a minute or two on the bridge, watching the traffic on the river and admiring the line of the waterfront on the north bank. It filled him with far more nostalgic joy than all the hills and valleys of Plumpton Bois. Near Scotland Yard a pavement artist greeted him by name.

'Mornin', Inspector.'

Cromwell, much to his surprise, threw him a shilling. He was usually careful with his money, but this morning he felt like throwing a reasonable part of it away.

He soon finished his business at the Yard and then went to his own room and rang through to enquire about the reactions of the War Office to his questions about John Henry Mellish and his wartime record under the alias of Walker. A typist brought him a minute of the conversation with official quarters. Apparently the War Office had been very helpful.

There was only one John Henry Walker on the 2nd Loamshires list. His record seemed to tally with what Cromwell had learned at Helsham. He had handled the difficulties of his enlistment very well. His description showed him to be a well set-up man in first class physical condition. He had given his date of birth as 1904 and when asked to produce his Identity Card, having found himself unable to overcome the difficulty of discrepancy in names, had explained that his real name was Walker, but that he was illegitimate and had been adopted by the Mellishes, who had registered him under their family name although he was known as John Henry Walker. He had no next of kin as he had lived away from his foster parents for years and didn't get on with them in any case. Taking some risk, although he had little to lose by it, he had suggested that the recruiting office might enquire at Helsham and confirm what he said. Apparently they had not followed it up. He had been enlisted under the name of Walker.

There followed a list of his misdeeds and convictions during his period of training. He had proved an apt soldier and had trained well and taken to the new life. He had, however, shown a wilful streak and a lack of discipline due, it was assumed, to his background and earlier life. He had been absent a time or two without leave, but had returned without an escort and taken his punishment cheerfully. There were reports of drunkenness and lack of respect for his superior officers. Finally, a theft of money and goods from a shop he had entered with a fellow private in Ipswich. Both the culprits had received short terms of imprisonment only, due to the fact that D-Day was imminent and every good soldier was required. There was a note that his companion in the burglary had been a younger man named Hough...

The name of Hough was quite familiar to Cromwell, but two subsequent paragraphs were more in his line.

One announced the death of John Henry Walker on the beaches on D-Day. The other stated, perhaps in view of the gallant end to his career, that during his service in the 2nd Loamshires he had fallen under the influence of a younger man who had been responsible for many of his misdemeanours, although never sharing in the punishments. The bad penny in Walker's life had been an old soldier and apparently knew his way about. His name and number were given. He was Oscar Fowler!

14

UNPLEASANT RECEPTION

When Littlejohn rang up Mr. Cunliffe for an appointment he received short shrift.

'I'm busy. You've already occupied enough of my time and I can't see that I can tell you anything more...'

'I'm sorry, sir, but I must insist. This is most important and recent developments make it essential that I see you.'

A pause.

'What developments?'

The voice was most unpleasant.

'I prefer not to discuss them over the telephone.'

'I don't see why not. However, you can call in before noon. You might be lucky to find me free. But I warn you, I can't give you much time.'

Cunliffe gave Littlejohn anything but a cordial welcome when he arrived at his office. He wore an air of suppressed rage. He didn't even offer him a seat, so Littlejohn helped himself to a chair facing the lawyer at his desk.

The room was old-fashioned like its occupant. Two windows with gauze screens bearing the names of the legal partnership in faded gilt overlooked the town square. A pile of japanned deed boxes, an old-fashioned roll-top desk closed in one corner. Mr. Cunliffe's business seemed too vast for the desk to cope with and he was seated at a large leather-topped table behind piles of deeds and documents. At his age, he surely was unable to deal with all that lot and Littlejohn assumed that it was a protective front behind which the ill-tempered solicitor entrenched himself. A few old padded Victorian chairs here and there and some Spy cartoons in dusty frames on the walls.

'I'm growing tired of the way this case is going, Superintendent. I'm inclined to agree that the crime was committed by some unknown burglar or passing tramp.'

The eyes were dim and malicious and the features the colour of parchment. Nevertheless, the old man seemed fit and mentally very alert. He was tough, like his old-time rival, Hubbard. It was difficult to imagine the pair of them passionately contending for the love of a woman who'd recently died unmarried at the age of eighty. Perhaps their malevolence for one another kept them alive.

'You told me, sir, that Miss Johnson's will distributed her estate between the late Cecil Savage and yourself. He got the property and you got the cash in the bank account...'

'Yes, yes. No need to go into that again...'

He paused and raised himself in his chair and leaned across the festoon of papers like a judge bestirring himself to address a prisoner. It made him look like a withered tortoise projecting himself from his shell.

'I believe you are quite a celebrity in the world of crime, Littlejohn. I wonder therefore at your wasting your time and mine in this sort of futile repetition. I've already gone into all that with you.'

The cold blue eyes behind rimless spectacles with thin gold side-pieces fixed themselves on the Superintendent without a flicker or a blink.

Littlejohn gave him a bland look in return.

'Since last you and I met, Mr. Cunliffe, much more information has come into my possession. Savage inherited the house and you the bank balance. Who inherited the rest?'

Cunliffe lowered himself behind his barricade of legal documents again and glared over the top of his spectacles.

'What do you mean by the rest?'

'The cash, totalling thirty thousand pounds, which Miss Johnson drew from the bank in notes after selling her securities some years ago.'

Dead silence. Cunliffe had never expected this. It shook his self-possession, because he'd no idea how much more Littlejohn knew. He parried it with another show of ill-temper.

'Who has told you about that? It's nothing whatever to do with your case. I suppose it's that boastful, loud-voiced Parkinson at the bank who's been divulging confidential information...'

'Had he not co-operated, we would have needed to obtain a court order instead.'

'Not so easy as you think. But you'll not find me as gullible as Parkinson, sir. I'm not to be bullied into betraying professional secrets.'

'I'm not asking you to do so. I already know all I need about Miss Johnson's affairs. I think my report will not only interest the Director of Public Prosecutions, but the Law Society as well, on the grounds of unprofessional conduct...'

Cunliffe's mouth moved in a nervous chewing motion. He lowered his head and quietly regarded the backs of his old-man's hands, knotted with hard blue veins and brittle-looking, folded on the table in front of him. He might have been estimating their capacity to strangle Littlejohn. Then he looked up and spoke quietly.

'You can't shake me with threats, Littlejohn. I'm too old to be afraid of that sort of thing. And you'd better be careful what you say or else I'll have to call in someone and ask you to repeat it.'

'I'm sure you wouldn't like anyone else present when I tell you what I've learned, sir. For example, the paternity of Miss Melody Johnson's illegitimate son, born in 1904...'

Cunliffe didn't explode or threaten. He rose and slowly walked to the window and looked out over the top of the gauze screen at the busy market place outside. Littlejohn noticed that he dragged one leg slightly on the way. When he turned and faced Littlejohn, he had grown paler, a sickly yellow.

'Go on...'

The snarl had left his voice. He sounded tired out. He wasn't sure of his ground and age was beginning to tell. He seemed to be searching in his mind for what Littlejohn might know and, at his time of life, he had a lot of recollections to turn over. Littlejohn got the impression of helplessness putting on a brave countenance and he was sorry for Cunliffe, still standing there as if wondering where to go next.

'I must remind you, Mr. Cunliffe, that I've no legal right to press questions and you can still show me the door. But I'd regard that as a hostile act and a desire to hide something...'

The eyes grew hard again for a moment.

'I said go on. No need to lay down the law to me. I know more than you about that.'

He returned to his chair and sat down. Then he poured himself a glass of water from a decanter at his elbow and drank it with a steady hand. He clasped his hands in front of him on the table again.

'Now. Ask me what you wish. I won't promise to answer. But if you're right in saying you know all about everything, it doesn't matter whether I answer or not, does it? Well...? Does it? First of all, though, tell me, am I the only one honoured by a visit from you on this matter or are you personally going from door to door in the neighbourhood asking questions?'

'You aren't the first I've visited, sir. I prefer not to say more. Most of the talk was personal and confidential.'

'Then you've been quizzing Hubbard, haven't you?'

He looked down at his hands again and didn't seem to expect an answer to his question. He spoke as though talking to himself.

'So, he's waited all this time for the right moment to strike me down. Well, it's too late. He's missed the boat and come to the wrong conclusion. Hubbard thinks I killed Savage, doesn't he?'

'Nothing was said to that effect, sir.'

'But implied. Do you believe that, too, Littlejohn?'

'No. I've reached no decision on the case yet, sir.'

'But you suspect me. You think I was at *Johnsons Place* rifling the safe in the cellar when Savage intruded. And that I killed him to avoid discovery. Well, I wasn't. There was no money in the safe at that time, and I knew it. I'm not pleading with you to believe me. But, in the interest of justice, of which I am a servant, and not to save my own neck, I'll tell you how I knew the safe was empty.'

He paused and gave Littlejohn a slow crafty smile.

'It was empty because I took away the money before Melody Johnson died.'

Cunliffe appeared to be the more surprised of the two of them. His bombshell had proved to be a damp squib. Littlejohn showed no astonishment.

'I thought that might perhaps be the case, sir. Maybe we'd better start at the beginning.'

'I'll do that, provided there's no intrusion in my private affairs.'

Littlejohn shrugged his shoulders.

'It seems to me it will be difficult to separate the two.'

Cunliffe made no reply. He thought for a moment, and then:

'About six years ago, Miss Johnson had her first stroke. She quickly recovered from it as regards the use of her limbs and her speech, but her brain must have suffered, for her personality changed. She and I had always been good friends...'

An understatement, but Cunliffe continued. In his prime, he must have been a good advocate in court. He spoke plainly and quickly, choosing his words, as though explaining a case.

'I visited Miss Johnson a number of times during her illnesses.

I was her solicitor, as well as her friend. Her mental change principally concerned her attitude towards money. She had a large proportion of her funds invested in good stocks and shares and before she became ill, must have worried about the decline in their capital value. Government stocks, for example, had depreciated disastrously since the war. Such things were bound to worry her. After her first brain haemorrhage, the matter grew into an obsession. Without consulting me, she sold most of her investments, and had the proceeds placed to her account at the bank. You learned that from Parkinson, I gather.'

Cunliffe frowned and tightened his lips as though such confidences were distasteful to him.

'So did I, at the time the transactions occurred. Parkinson rang me up in a fearful panic. I pretended I was familiar with what was going on. But I wasn't. I knew as little about it as Parkinson. I was shocked.'

He didn't look it. He went on in an impersonal and objective way as though he were enlightening the bench on an intricate case.

'At the time, I was engaged on a very exacting High Court matter. *Regina v. Meager*. Remember it?'

A case of murder, which had eventually been reduced to manslaughter. Littlejohn remembered it well. So, Cunliffe must have been solicitor for the accused. A very clever defence.

'I hadn't time to call and see Miss Johnson. I was travelling to London and back a lot. So I wrote to her and told her to take no further steps until she'd seen me. I was too late, however. She had already bought a safe and installed it in the cellar, where you and I saw it, drawn the money from the bank, and stuffed it in the safe. When I visited her after the Meager case was over, there it all was. Almost thirty thousand pounds in banknotes. I tried to persuade her to re-invest it, or at least, put it back in the bank for safety. But she was obsessed by the security of her money and declined.

She further embarrassed me by giving me a duplicate key of the safe in her cellar.'

'Excuse me. A matter which arises from what you have just said. You said you wrote to Miss Johnson?'

'Yes.'

'When you came to sort out her affairs after her death, did you bring away from the house any papers, any correspondence? Perhaps including the letters you and the bank wrote to her about the danger of having so much cash about the house.'

'Yes. She had always been a careful, tidy woman. She had not, of course, kept all her letters, but certain important ones she received were there, in her desk, placed back in their envelopes and tied up in three bundles with what appeared to be pink corset tape. I went through the lot and retained the ones she had thus filed. I intended going through them, reading them again and then destroying them. The residue... bills, accounts and the like which had been paid and receipted, I left where I found them, in the drawers.'

'Thank you. You have the letters you brought away from *Johnsons Place* still in your possession, Mr. Cunliffe?'

'Yes. They are locked in one of those deed boxes over there. Why?'

'I would be grateful if you would lend me a few selected ones which I'd choose before I go. I'd like to have a look over them for fingerprints.'

'Whatever for? Do you think Sarah Rasp could have been reading her mistress's correspondence? She was the only one who had access to it at that time.'

'All the same, I'd be grateful...'

'All right. But let me get on with my tale. It's lunch time. I didn't... I couldn't press the matter of the money she was keeping on the premises. After all, Miss Johnson was just recovering from a stroke. I didn't wish to worry her into another attack. So, I decided to wait until later. Instead, she had another stroke before

I could raise the problem. Two years later, another cerebral haemorrhage, like the first one. She recovered again. But this time, she'd a fresh worry on her mind. She was sure she'd die if she had yet another attack. She was anxious about her will.'

Cunliffe paused. Then he continued cautiously.

'She had no near relatives around her. There had been, as you discovered, an illegitimate son. His paternity is no affair of yours and does not affect this case...'

Cunliffe was a cool one. He skated insolently over what must have been his own love affair with Melody Johnson and all the disastrous effects it had had on her life and probably on his own as well. It might have been a mere, almost irrelevant item in a lawsuit he was conducting. He went on unemotionally. Perhaps time and the damping down, the hardening of his feelings, along with his arteries, by age, were his allies.

'There was also her brother, Benjamin Quincey Johnson, who ran away from her home in his early twenties and was never heard of again, unaccounted for. The only remaining member of the Johnson family on whom hands could be laid was Cyril Savage, Miss Johnson's great-nephew, whom she despised. I don't know why. She said she had only met him twice and then in his infancy. He was then a horrible little child and that impression remained with her for the rest of her days. Savage had tried to establish friendly contact with his aunt, but she would have none of it. She felt the interest he took in her was purely financial. She left him her house and its contents in her will and nothing else.'

'The contents of which, I presume, would have included the cash in the safe.'

Cunliffe glared at Littlejohn over the top of his spectacles. He might have been interrupting a case before a judge.

'Please don't interrupt. This story is long enough without making it into a discussion. I was just about to say, the will was executed before Miss Johnson turned her investments into cash and put the money away in the safe on the premises. I saw at once the implications. Unless something was done before her death, Savage would inherit the lot. I had to act. Miss Johnson's physical and mental condition after her second stroke precluded her from properly dealing with the routine of her finances, including the mass of money in the cellar. It fell to me to handle her day to day business, pay her bills, provide ready money. I called every week and did this.'

Cunliffe's hands now began to tremble and his voice grew husky. He took another drink of water, polished his spectacles and seemed better for the pause.

A middle-aged woman entered and stood like an army private waiting for permission to speak.

'Well? What is it?'

'It's one o'clock, Mr. Cunliffe. What about your lunch?'

The old man flapped his hands petulantly.

'I shan't be able to go to the club today. Damned nuisance. I'm just in the middle of something very involved. Telephone the club and tell 'em I won't be in... Cook me a poached egg on toast and make me some tea in half an hour...'

'Now, perhaps we can proceed... There had been thirty thousand pounds in the safe originally. On Miss Johnson's instructions, I used five thousand of that to provide an annuity for Sarah Rasp. She had been with the family for almost sixty years and Miss Johnson wished to make provision for her. Luckily, Miss Johnson didn't die before the scheduled limit for such gifts *inter vivos* had run, so Sarah's bequest will not bear death duties.'

This must have been the 'present' mentioned by Sarah to Littlejohn, but she mustn't have known Cunliffe was concerned with it.

The interview seemed interminable. Littlejohn was as anxious as Cunliffe had said *he* was to get it over, yet the lawyer resisted all interruptions and seemed lost in the ramifications of his narrative.

'Excuse me, sir. Did you make any enquiries about Miss Johnson's son or her brother?'

'Yes. I advertised many times for Benjamin without results. It was a forlorn hope and, after all this time, we can only assume that he is dead. As for the son, I visited the orphanage which arranged his adoption. I had extreme difficulty in obtaining even the least information about him. He had been adopted by some people called Mellish in the village where the institution stands. He had, it seems, left the place to join the army at the outbreak of the last war. His record, I was told, was not a good one. After joining up, he disappeared from view. Whether or not he was killed, I couldn't ascertain. They had no record of it and his name is not on the orphanage War Memorial.'

'He enlisted as J. H. Walker, sir. He was killed in the Normandy landings.'

Cunliffe's mouth slackened slightly and he looked down at his trembling hands. His shoulders sagged momentarily. Then he sighed as though somehow relieved. The only signs that the loss of his son had affected him. He was himself again almost at once.

'How did you know that?'

'Our investigating force is probably larger than yours, sir. We combed the whole locality for information.'

'I thought he might perhaps have died. Did you know that Mellish, as he was called, found out who his mother was?'

Littlejohn must have shown surprise, for the lawyer gave him a glance of triumph.

'You didn't? Well, I did. When I called at the orphanage and talked to that garrulous old ass of a warden there, he gave me as an example of young Mellish's character, details of how he'd broken in the muniments room, rummaged among the records and found his own particulars, which he left on a table and thus incriminated himself. It was during the war when he brazenly returned to his old haunts with a pal and broke in the orphanage and stole money and some silver sports cups. He had not only left his file lying accusingly about, but liberally sprinkled fingerprints around. The police were soon on his trail and he was arrested. In view of the fact that he was shortly going abroad into action and that he was an old boy of the institution, the case was not pressed. But Mellish died knowing who his mother was.'

Cunliffe suddenly looked tired and harassed. He seemed drained of energy and had lost the thread of his story.

'Would you rather I returned after lunch, sir?'

Cunliffe accepted the question as a challenge and suddenly perked-up.

'No! I've wasted enough time on you already. I'm not going into an afternoon session.'

Littlejohn brought the discussion back to realities again.

'So, Mrs. Savage, as widow of Miss Johnson's only surviving next-of-kin at her death, will inherit the cash after all, as though the estate were intestate?'

Cunliffe didn't challenge Littlejohn's point of law.

'Yes.'

'What happened to the remaining cash after Sarah Rasp's annuity had been paid for?'

'What was left I placed in the bank. Not Parkinson's bank. He's too inquisitive and indiscreet. It is banked in a client's account of my firm. I will deal with it and see that it reaches its lawful destination.'

'Twenty-five thousand pounds?'

'No! What do you think Miss Johnson lived on for six years? After she sold her securities, she got no dividends. She had to live on her capital. Although it has nothing to do with you, I'll tell you that there was eighteen thousand pounds or thereabouts left. When I took over Miss Johnson's financial affairs, I decided at once to remove the money from the cellar. I first opened the safe with the duplicate key in our hands and compiled a rough statement as to what had been spent since the securities were sold and what should have remained. Approximately, two thousand pounds could not be accounted for. With Miss Johnson ill we could not question her closely and even had we been able to do so, her mental state was past remembering details of what she had spent, lost or given away since she acquired the cash.'

'Do you think the money was stolen?'

'How do I know? I thoroughly investigated the matter, but it got me nowhere. Sarah Rasp swore she'd not taken it nor did she know where it had gone. Miss Johnson seemed confused and I couldn't get a sensible answer out of her. Sarah Rasp mentioned an attempted burglary, but the burglar hadn't even got in the place.'

'Burglary? When was that?'

'Roughly four years ago. Sarah Rasp woke one night and heard someone prowling around the house. She put on the lights and telephoned the police. She must have scared off the intruder. Probably a passing tramp. He'd forced the window in the pantry but hadn't got inside the house. Miss Johnson wasn't told of the matter. She was ill at the time and it would have done no good to upset her. I arrranged for the police to keep an eye on the place in future, for a time, Sarah Rasp kept a noisy dog which had eventually to be disposed of as it used to bark incessantly. And now, is that all? Because I haven't had my lunch yet and I'm hungry.'

'Just one more question, sir. What made Savage pay his first visit to *Johnsons Place* without the company of you or one of your clerks?'

'He was a stupid fool. We'd already made an appointment for somebody from this office to accompany him. But Savage couldn't wait. He turned-up, without warning us, five days before we expected him. Made the excuse he'd got the day off. I was engaged at the time and the estate clerk, with my reluctant permission and after identifying Savage, gave him the key to *Johnsons Place* and told him how to find it. If Savage hadn't been in such an ungodly hurry, he'd have been alive today.'

'Was *Johnsons Place* left empty from the time Miss Johnson died and Sarah Rasp went away until the present, sir?'

'No. That is a damp valley and the house is damp in consequence. I wished someone to keep an eye on it and light a fire or two there every other day if the weather was rainy. I paid Penkethman, the farmer at the place about a quarter of a mile higher up the valley, to act as temporary caretaker. He and his wife are decent, conscientious people and were to be relied on to do the job properly and be honest about the contents of the house. From what I can gather locally, they hardly let the place out of their sight. They're made that way. Eccentric, suspicious and honest to the last penny.'

Littlejohn could well imagine it. They were reputed to watch their own property almost day and night when it was threatened by intruders.

'A strange thing,' he said. 'They happened to be both in Povington when Savage arrived at *Johnsons Place*. Someone else also arrived and was there when Savage suddenly turned up. The murder took place at the very time when the house wasn't being watched.'

Littlejohn collected the letters Mr. Cunliffe had promised he could take away for examination, bade the lawyer good-bye, and thanked him and left just as the poached eggs on toast were being brought in.

15

INTRUDER IN THE DARK

The Chief Constable of Povington was surprised and disappointed by the letter he found among the post on his desk when he arrived at nine o'clock for his round of daily duties. He called in Superintendent Harris and flung it across his desk to him.

'Read that.'

A feline look spread over Harris's face as he perused it. Then, he carefully folded the letter, slipped it in its envelope and handed it back.

'It seems Littlejohn's been converted to my original theory about Savage's murder. It's taken him long enough to find out. And that leaves us where we started...'

The letter was in Littlejohn's own hand and posted in Plumpton on the previous day.

After careful investigation and interviewing all those who might give useful information, I have come to the conclusion that the crime was probably committed by some stranger, perhaps a tramp or a professional thief, who, finding Johnsons Place *empty and unguarded broke in and was ransacking the place when Savage arrived and disturbed him. I suggest the work of Superintendent Harris be continued and the search for strangers who might have been in the locality be pursued ...*

My colleague and I will be returning to London tomorrow afternoon, subject to your concurrence, after I have completed my detailed report for you. On our way, we will call on you and hand over the key of the premises. We will lock up the place and leave all secure and, when I see you, I will discuss with you the advisability of placing the house under guard ...

Superintendent Harris preened himself.

'It seems all the clever ones aren't at Scotland Yard, sir. We county police can teach them a thing or two sometimes. I like the way Littlejohn says he's calling to advise us on what to do when he's gone.'

The Chief was nettled.

'No need to rub it in, Harris. I know I was responsible for calling in the Yard.'

'I wasn't...'

'But why write a letter? A waste of his time and ours, if as he says, he's calling here on his way home. I must confess I'm disappointed. If this is the way famous Scotland Yard officers work, we'll rely on our own staff in future.'

The conference of commiseration was interrupted by the intrusion of a young and nervous constable. He'd already knocked on the door and received no answer.

'Yes? What is it, Gadgett? Can't you see the Chief Constable and I are busy?'

'Yes, sir. But I thought I'd better interrupt, as it's important. Superintendent Littlejohn has just arrived.'

'Already!'

'Yes, sir.'

The young bobby's eyes were popping with excitement. He could hardly get out his words. It rattled Harris to think that a Scotland Yard detective who, to his way of thinking, had been a failure, could stimulate such enthusiasm.

'He's called early. Probably wants to get it over,' he said to his Chief.

He turned on Gadgett.

'Well, Gadgett. What are you waiting for? Show him in.'

'All of them, sir?'

'What do you mean, all of them? Is there a procession?'

'In a way, sir, yes. Green's with him, and Inspector Cromwell. They've made an arrest in connection with the Plumpton Bois murder. They've got a man in handcuffs...'

After leaving Cunliffe's office, Littlejohn met Cromwell, as arranged, for a report and lunch at the hotel across the square. Cromwell had already eaten when the Superintendent arrived and Littlejohn at once gave him the letters he'd borrowed from the lawyer. Cromwell then left for London where they were to be examined right away.

Littlejohn settled down to a good meal himself. After that, he returned to Plumpton police station and wrote a long letter to the Chief Constable in Povington. Then he lit his pipe and strode to the post office, bought some stamps, asked about the time it would take for a letter posted then in Plumpton, to reach Povington and was assured by Mrs. Fowler that it would be delivered first post the next morning.

Mrs. Fowler was busy weighing and making-up pound packets of sultanas in the grocery department. She greeted him shyly, replied to his enquiries, and said her husband was out about his business of collecting the mail from the various boxes.

Cromwell returned at seven that evening and they ate a good meal together. Over coffee, Cromwell gave Littlejohn a full report from the technical staff at the Yard, where the exhibits he had taken there had been carefully examined.

At nine o'clock they took a stroll round the village, called at the police station, found Green was at home, and gave him some instructions. He saw them to the gate, where they surprised him by shaking hands as they bade him good night. He returned to his wife in great spirits.

'They both shook hands with me. They must appreciate what I've done on the case.'

The detectives were back at the *Miners Arms* by ten o'clock. There, they told Crabb they would be returning to London early next day and would like their bills immediately after breakfast.

'Found the murderer already?'

Crabb smelled strongly of whisky and was garrulous.

'No. But our work here is finished. The rest is a matter of wait and see. We think some vagrant or other passing through might have done it. We'll be retiring at once, ready for an early breakfast about eight o'clock.'

'I'll tell the missus. If you ask me, the crime will never be solved...'

'But we haven't asked you, have we?'

Crabb recoiled hurt and hastily left them. They saw him unsteadily entering the taproom where the locals gathered every evening. It was obvious he was eager to break the news in as uncomplimentary a manner as he could.

At half past eleven, the neon sign which decorated the front of the hotel was extinguished. At the same time, the half-dozen lights which illuminated the village street were automatically switched off. Crabb had already staggered to bed and Littlejohn and Cromwell, waiting in the dark in Cromwell's room, heard Mrs. Crabb's weary footsteps ascending to the family quarters on the top floor.

Cromwell quietly opened the door and peered out. The hotel was in total darkness. He tapped Littlejohn on the shoulder and the pair of them, carrying their shoes, silently descended and quietly let themselves out into the night. They sat on the seat by the door and put on their shoes again.

All was silent in the village. They could hear, in the distance, the stream rattling over the stones. Somewhere in the vicinity a stable-clock, ahead of time, struck twelve. There were odd lights here and there in some of the houses. The doctor seemed to have visitors. There were two cars parked in the road by his gate, and two of the rooms of the house were illuminated.

At the end of the byroad leading to *Johnsons Place* they were met by Green, whose uniformed silhouette, exaggerated conspiratorial gestures, and general bearing reminded Littlejohn of a bobby in *The Pirates of Penzance*. Drawing his two fellow conspirators in a huddle, he hoarsely whispered to them.

'I've been watching the place for nearly two hours and nobody's turned up yet.'

Stabbing the darkness with his forefinger, he indicated Penkethman's farm. There was a light in one of the upper rooms with a drawn blind between.

'The watchers are at it up at Penkethman's,' he said.

Littlejohn wondered if the Penkethmans kept vigil in shifts or together.

Littlejohn unlocked the door with his key and they entered the house, guided by the small torch Cromwell carried. In the dark and damp the house was even more forbidding. In the intermittent silences, they could hear water dripping somewhere from a softly hissing ball-tap and it was gently echoed outside the house as it overflowed from the tank. Mice scuttered away as they passed from room to room on the ground floor. Finally, the three policemen took up their quarters in the dining-room where Mrs. Savage had waited helplessly whilst her husband was being murdered.

Littlejohn looked at the illuminated dial of his watch. It was a quarter past midnight. Green rummaged under his coat and brought out some bulky packages which he laid on the table. One was a vacuum flask.

'Coffee,' he said in a whisper which seemed to come from deep down in his body. 'We'll have some when you feel like it, sir.'

Cromwell felt like drinking the lot right away. The soup at

dinner had been over-salted and he was suffering from mild hallucinations in which cool beer and sweet tea figured largely. However, he thanked Green for his kindly foresight. This seemed to stimulate the bobby to further efforts. He indicated another group of packets.

'Beef sandwiches.'

Excusing himself, Green switched on his own muffled torch and began to potter about softly. His boots creaked. He seemed familiar with the house, for he quickly gathered cups and plates from drawers and set them out as though they were attending a garden-party instead of a vigil for a murderer. They must have been from Miss Johnson's best service, for they were the kind now found in antique shops instead of kitchens. Green wiped them all carefully on a cloth which he conjured from another drawer. It was obvious that in the course of his constabulary duties since Miss Johnson's death, he had partaken of his refreshments there before. He set out the sandwiches and poured out the coffee the aroma of which seemed to fill the house.

'Please help yourselves, gentlemen. We might as well fortify ourselves before the fun begins, mightn't we?'

It spoke much for Green's discretion and discipline that he hadn't even asked what the fun was to be. All he'd been told was to meet Littlejohn and Cromwell near *Johnsons Place*. He'd guessed the rest.

They ate their picnic almost in silence, Cromwell now and then flashing his torch so that they could see what they were eating. During the interim dark spells they could hear one another chewing appreciatively and the sounds of Green's heavy breathing. When it was over, Green carried the cups and plates and himself away and could be heard rinsing them in the back quarters. He reappeared with his clean dishes and replaced them where he'd found them. Then they waited again for what seemed hours in the darkness. The mice returned now and then for the crumbs of their feast and Green repelled them until they grew quite tame and ignored his muffled dismissals.

They spoke in brief whispers. Finally, Green seemed to get impatient.

'I wonder if he's here already, behind the cellar door, like he was with Savage...'

Then he paused.

'Somebody's coming,' he said.

Littlejohn and Cromwell couldn't hear anything. Green must have had very sensitive hearing, for the intruder was upon them almost before they realised it. The garden gate slowly creaked, there was a pause, and then a human form like a shadow appeared against the background of the night outside.

It was no longer pitch dark. The air had cleared, stars were shining and through the window they could make out the newcomer's face.

'Good Lord!' hissed Green.

'Shhh... He's got what looks like a nylon stocking over his head and face.'

Which was right. The face, just visible, was like that of a nightmare figure in a waxworks show. Two holes for eyes, a bulge where the nose should be, and the rest a shapeless grey mass.

Lest Green should prove too enthusiastic, Littlejohn thought it well to give him a word of warning.

'Don't make a move, until I give the word. Remember, Green, this man's a murderer.'

'Very good, sir.'

And Green whipped out his truncheon and stood at the ready.

The visitor didn't hesitate. He might have been returning to his own home after a night out. He made straight for the front door, produced a key, unlocked it, entered and snapped on a torch. The door creaked back and, as though sensing danger, the newcomer stood a moment on the threshold to listen. Then he moved silently, the pencil of light from his torch marking his progress along the hall, right to the cellar door.

'Right,' said Littlejohn.

Cromwell switched on the large electric lamp he'd brought with him and the light fell full on the surprised figure at the top of the cellar steps. He was clad in an old dark suit, a muffler, and he wore gloves. His head and face were hidden in a mask of nylon stocking; there was a ladder in the material across one of his cheeks. He reached swiftly and struck at Cromwell's elbow with his fist. The lamp clattered to the floor and went out. Almost before darkness had fallen on them again, there was a fresh light from Green's torch. The visitor turned his expressionless face in the constable's direction and raised his arm again. But Green got his blow in first. His truncheon descended like a railway signal giving the all-clear on top of his assailant's head and laid him out.

Green grunted with hesitant satisfaction. He hoped he hadn't killed him. The man was struggling uncertainly to his feet, however, and still showing signs of pugnacity.

'Shall I...?' asked Green.

'Handcuffs. Yes.'

Green had them on his quarry before he knew what was happening. Only the eyes expressed the feelings of the victim, almost protruding from the mask with fearful hate.

Littlejohn dragged the stocking from the hidden head and face.

It was Fowler, the postman.

Green was flabbergasted. Nobody ever knew whom he had expected to find there. All the postman's wrath seemed concentrated on the uniformed rival he had always hated.

'You bloody bullying copper, Green! You're only any good when you've got your truncheon and the other chap's not armed...'

And he made a sudden effort to butt Green in the chest. This time Green slapped him across the face with the back of his hand and Fowler measured his length again on the carpet. But the stuffing wasn't all out of him yet. In spite of his plight he tried to look at his ease.

'I was taking a walk. I saw a light on here. That's all. Only natural I should call and see what was happening.'

'Walking out at this time of night, and letting yourself in the house with a key? And wearing a mask? Come along. We'll finish all this at the police station.'

They hadn't a vehicle handy and, as Fowler continued to be violently unco-operative, Cromwell and Green had to frog-march him to his destination.

Mrs. Green was waiting for them with all the lights on. In the midst of the surrounding darkness of the silent village, the police station looked like a lighthouse in full glow. Fowler declined abusively Green's polite offer of a chair. He seemed more put-out by Green's obvious triumph than by the fact that he'd been caught red-handed. They sat him on the hearthrug. Green held him and Cromwell searched his pockets. There was nothing very exciting at first about what came to light. A second torch, a tool like a burglar's jemmy, a cosh, and a bunch of keys, some of which, after examination, Littlejohn guessed were those of the front door of *Johnsons Place* and of the safe in the cellar. Then, in his waistcoat pocket, a gold watch without a chain. Littlejohn examined it and nodded and placed it on the table with the rest of the contents.

In the room behind, there were sounds of crockery being assembled and then a whistling kettle started to boil. Mrs. Green was preparing her customary refreshments.

'I want my lawyer,' spluttered Fowler.

He was an unpleasant sight. Never prepossessing, unkempt and half-washed, he now looked worse than ever. His adventures of earlier in the night, the dishevelling results of removing his mask, and the pallor from his present rage combined to give him a clown's angry face under a shock of golliwog hair.

'At this time of night? Who *is* your lawyer?'

'Mr. Cunliffe, of Povington.'

It may have been true, or else Fowler might have been trying to think of the most unpleasant lawyer he knew.

'You'll have to wait till a more reasonable hour. Meanwhile, you will be detained here in custody and removed to Povington later.'

'You're not getting anything out of me. I won't answer any questions without a lawyer. And when I tell my solicitor what's happened to me tonight, Green, your number's up in the police force.'

'We don't propose to question you, Fowler, just now. But I must warn you that we will take you to Povington as soon as possible and there you will be charged with attempted burglary at *Johnsons Place*. I must add that you need say nothing more, but anything you say may be taken down and used in evidence...'

'Attempted burglary...?'

Fowler looked relieved and almost said 'Is that all?', but changed his mind.

'Yes. Lock him in the cells, Green.'

Fowler looked ready to resist again, but Green was implacable and he eventually went off like a lamb. They could hear them tramping down the stone stairs to the solitary underground cell and the gate clanged to. Green reappeared.

'He's asking for his supper.'

'He can go hungry. He ought to have had a meal before he set out on his nocturnal prowl. This is no time for preparing refreshment for him. He can have his breakfast at Povington. And if he creates any disturbance, don't pander to him. Let him exhaust himself.'

'He won't disturb the youngsters. They're in the attics.'

Mrs. Green entered, hot and smiling in spite of the late hour. She was carrying a large tray filled to capacity with sandwiches, scones, fancy cakes and Swiss and jam roll. In the middle of the lot, the huge family teapot. There was enough for a Sunday School picnic.

Full to capacity under the persuasions of Mrs. Green, Littlejohn and Cromwell finally left the constable and his wife to their own devices and made off to the *Miners Arms*. The stable-clock struck two in the darkness. The door of the hotel was unlocked as they had left it. Crabb's snores echoed down the staircase. They entered quietly and parted at their bedroom doors to get as much sleep as they could.

16

BRIEF RESISTANCE

Before the police could question or charge Fowler, a dramatic interlude broke into their discussions.

It was reported from the home of Mr. Jeremiah Cunliffe that he had been found dead in his study that morning from an overdose of sleeping tablets.

Young Cunliffe himself telephoned.

'I thought I ought to report it personally and at once. The doctor is here and says there's no doubt about the cause of death and an official post mortem will doubtless confirm his own findings.

'My uncle was found less than an hour ago sitting in his chair beside the cold fire. Mrs. Cunliffe and he occupied separate bedrooms and, as he often stayed up late at night reading or going through business papers, my aunt was not alarmed when he didn't come upstairs before she fell asleep. She takes her breakfast in bed and it was only when the daily help arrived and entered his study around nine o'clock that his death was discovered. You'll be sending someone to the house right away, I suppose. I haven't yet informed the coroner. I'll leave that to you, now. Nothing has been touched in the study, except, of course, any disturbances which the doctor had, of necessity, to make...'

He sounded quite cheerful, as well he might. He'd been waiting for twenty years or more to take over as principal partner of the firm.

The Chief Constable repeated the message to Littlejohn, and then paused for his reaction.

'You don't seem very surprised, Superintendent.'

'I'm not, sir. I interviewed old Mr. Cunliffe yesterday. From what he told me, I suspected that he had been guilty of grave professional misconduct. Among other things, he had removed a sum of about twenty thousand pounds in cash from Miss Johnson's private safe at *Johnsons Place*. He told me he had done so for safety and with Miss Johnson's concurrence and had placed it to the credit of his firm's client's account and would be dealing with it when he came to disburse Miss Johnson's estate. I fear, however, that he might have misappropriated the funds and when matters are looked into, it will be revealed that he used the cash either to pay off his own debts or else to put the falsified books of his firm in order...'

'Good Lord! Old Cunliffe? He was regarded locally as a model of integrity.'

'A man can be pushed too far, sir. I hear his wife is extremely extravagant and they live in a lavish way. So much so, that at the age of over eighty, Cunliffe found himself unable to let-up, to say nothing of retiring.'

'This will cause a local scandal when the news gets out. And what about the murder of Savage? Had Cunliffe anything to do with that?'

'Not directly, I think. He had, even before Miss Johnson's death, removed her money, which, as her lawyer, she had more or less entrusted to him. He had, in his position as trustee, contrived, I fancy, to hide all traces of its existence. He had hoped to pass on the appropriate legacy to Savage, namely the house and its contents, and the will bequeathed the cash in the bank, which was only small, to Cunliffe for his services as trustee and as Miss Johnson's friend. The large hidden amount of cash had, as I said before, been spirited away by Cunliffe, the sole executor, who presumably took out probate without declaring the hoard. He hoped to get clean away with it. However, someone killed Savage and the whole Johnson position was then thrown wide open and investigated by the police. I told Cunliffe point-blank yesterday that we had traced the existence of Miss Johnson's fortune in cash and I asked him what had become of it. He was thus faced with an early disclosure of his conduct of the estate. He chose not to suffer disgrace and certain imprisonment.'

There was a silence.

'Had we better have Fowler in now, Littlejohn? I take it you're proposing to charge him with the murder of Savage.'

'Yes, sir. Shall I outline the case before Fowler appears or...?'

'Do it in front of Fowler. He hasn't confessed, has he?'

'Far from it. He also demands to see his lawyer before he answers any questions.'

'Who might his lawyer be?'

'Old Cunliffe.'

'No!'

Fowler was brought in.

The constable with him was red in the face.

'He's been giving trouble, sir. Demands to see his lawyer right away. Says he won't answer questions or even eat his breakfast until he's had his solicitor's advice.'

The Chief Constable nodded in Littlejohn's direction.

'He's all yours, Superintendent.'

'First of all, Fowler, I'm sorry your lawyer isn't available. He died early this morning.'

Fowler was visibly shaken. He looked awful. His night's escapades had not improved his appearance. His hatchet face was pale and unshaven and his eyes glowed feverishly in their deep orbits. He had been to bed fully dressed and his clothes looked to have come straight out of a ragbag.

'I don't believe it. You're trying to trick me. I insist on seeing Mr. Jeremiah Cunliffe right away.'

'It's true. You'll have to choose another solicitor.'

'I don't know any other.'

'I'm sure you don't. You only knew Mr. Cunliffe through your familiarity with his name on the letters to and from Miss Melody Johnson which you steamed open and read.'

In spite of his pitiable appearance, Fowler showed no signs of despair. He denied he'd ever done such a thing.

'Don't try to lie your way out of it, Fowler. I'll go so far as to say that every letter you collect or deliver in Plumpton is steamed open before it leaves the post office and read by you if you think it's of any importance. For years you've been reading Miss Johnson's correspondence...'

'That's a lie. You're trying to discredit me in front of these other gentlemen...'

'Don't deny it. Many envelopes, particularly those which passed between Miss Johnson and Mr. Cunliffe have been technically examined. Without exception they were found by our experts to have been steamed open and then stuck down again with a gum quite different from that originally on the envelope. The same will have happened, I've no doubt, to the letter I purposely wrote last night to the Chief Constable here. I must have surprised him by telling him I was throwing in my hand and returning to London forthwith. That was for your benefit alone, Fowler. You read it and took the bait. You arrived hot-foot at *Johnsons Place* after dark for another search for the money before my suggestion that the house be guarded was put into effect.'

'You can't prove a thing.'

Fowler seemed to have lapsed into a kind of apathy. The

discovery of his tricks had temporarily taken some of the steam out of him.

'I can prove all I'm telling you. Let's begin at the beginning, shall we? You met a certain John Henry Walker during your army service in the last war. His real name was Mellish...'

'Never heard of him. You've got the wrong chap if you think I ever knew a man by that name.'

'Among the property removed from your pockets last night, Fowler, was a gold watch inscribed *To A. M. from P. J. L. for long and faithful service*. That watch once belonged to John Henry Mellish's foster-father. John Henry stole it when he left home. It appears you, Fowler, stole it from John Henry.'

'I didn't. He gave it to me. We sort of swopped watches by way of keepsakes. Get me?'

'So you did know Walker or Mellish. You were in the army together. In fact, you were his evil genius. He was a ne'er-do-well, but you made him worse. You even induced him to rob the orphanage where he was placed as a baby. It was near the home of his foster-parents. Besides burgling the place, Walker turned up the records and found out who his real family were. He told you he'd discovered that he was the illegitimate son of Miss Melody Johnson, of *Johnsons Place*, Plumpton Bois. You made a mental note of it for future use. You'd already smelled blackmail, I'm sure.'

'That's not true. You're making it all up so you can pin the murder on me. What if Walker was a wrong 'un and did a bit of burgling now and then?' It doesn't follow that I was in it with him. You're not catching me out that way.'

Fowler spoke in a hoarse voice. It was obvious he was losing ground in the argument and now he wondered exactly how much the police knew of him and his past.

'I'm not trying to catch you out, or even asking you to say a word. We have proof for all this and can produce our witnesses when they are needed, even from among your old comrades in the army. You got as much information as you could out of J. H. Walker ready for a good round of pickings when you both got out of the army. But Walker was killed. It might have been a good thing if it had been you instead. You had all the field to yourself after that. I've no doubt you explored the neighbourhood of Plumpton Bois as soon as you could and asked about Miss Johnson as well. You found there was a vacancy for a postman there and you managed to get the job. This enabled you to settle and gave you a heaven-sent opportunity to find out more about your victim by steaming open and reading her correspondence. If you hadn't got the job there, it would have been just the same. You would have found it more difficult perhaps but you were ingenious enough to overcome that.'

Fowler was almost in a panic now. He licked his dry lips and asked for a drink to gain time. They gave him water which he accepted with gestures of disgust.

'I haven't had any breakfast.'

'You'll get it when we've finished.'

Littlejohn pursued his way relentlessly.

'You started your attack on Miss Johnson by writing her a letter supposed to come from her illegitimate son, begging and distressed. You told her where to address the money for which you asked. How did you induce her to keep the business secret and not tell a soul? Did you tell her, writing as her son, that you were on the run from the police?'

'You tell me. You seem to know all about it. I'm not helping you. I told you before I started that I wanted a lawyer.'

'It was easy for you, as postman, to intercept the letters containing the money. A very ingenious method of extortion. How much did you get in all? Two thousand? Three...?'

Fowler didn't say a word. He was staring straight in front of him, his hand contracting and jerking as though the tension was becoming a torture.

'Don't say it was a lie. It has been proved. I'm making-up none of this. The witnesses will be produced in due course. Then, you had a perfect windfall, Fowler. Letters, which you steamed open and read as usual, began to arrive disclosing a fabulous surprise. Miss Johnson, attacked by senile dementia, was converting her securities into cash. Thirty thousand pounds arriving at *Johnsons Place* ready to your hand. Not only that, but the makers of the safe Miss Johnson bought to contain it, sent a duplicate key by registered post for you to have copied and smooth your way. You couldn't wait. You hurried off to burgle the place as fast as your legs would take you. In your hurry you wakened Sarah Rasp and failed in your first attempt. After that the security of *Johnsons Place* was tightened up. P.C. Green began to keep an eye on it. Miss Johnson's illness necessitated night nursing, the doctor was often there, and to add to your troubles, Sarah Rasp got a dog, which, although not much in the way of a fighting guard, nevertheless roused the whole place with its yapping whenever there was an intrusion...'

There was a sudden interruption. Mrs. Fowler, dressed up to the nines, had arrived to demand what they were doing to her husband. She had, she said, retired to bed with him on the previous night, fallen asleep, and when she woke at four on the following morning, he'd vanished into thin air. Alarmed by his non-appearance when the mail arrived, she'd enquired at the police station and been told he'd been arrested and taken to Povington.

Mrs. Fowler's main concern was for Her Majesty's mail. It hadn't been collected, as usual, from the boxes and the deliveries hadn't been made in the village and were piling-up.

'I'll have to report it to the head postmaster if he's not coming back at once. They'll have to send a relief man. Will my husband be long?'

She was deposited in a small room and given a cup of tea. When informed that her husband would be detained for quite a while, she insisted on telephoning the head postmaster at once.

179

Only then did she seem more interested in her spouse. She asked to see him and this being refused for the time being, she said she couldn't wait as the post office was closed and that was really illegal. They sent her home in a police car.

When told of his wife's interference and the message she'd left, Fowler showed great annoyance and his spirits seemed to revive from it. He asked what she wanted to butt-in for and told them to keep her away as she knew nothing of his private affairs.

The Chief Constable was growing impatient. He gave instructions that they weren't on any account to be disturbed until the conference was over.

'Please resume, Littlejohn.'

Fowler was as white as a sheet. His face was drawn, his narrow nostrils quivering, his lips tight and pale. He was expecting the worst now and watched Littlejohn with anxious hostile eyes.

Littlejohn resumed rather rapidly.

'Matters didn't improve even after Miss Johnson's death. Sarah Rasp stayed on at the house until she'd made other personal arrangements. She left for her sister's only a short time before the premature arrival of Savage. After she went, the lawyer, Cunliffe, took on the Penkethmans as temporary custodians. Their farm was the nearest habitation to *Johnsons Place* and even the small payment Cunliffe offered them for their duties was welcome to that greedy pair. They gave him good value for his money. They did the job properly. They were used to guarding their farm from thieves and interlopers and the routine was second nature to them. One never knew at what time of day or night one would stumble across them. They treated *Johnsons Place* as though it was their own. They revelled in their work. In addition, they had a guard dog which, though benevolent to the average intruder, became savage at the sight of uniforms. It particularly hated Green and Fowler. Faced by all these obstacles, Fowler thought he'd never get another chance of burgling *Johnsons Place* for the hidden treasure before it was discovered by someone else. You see, Cunliffe, when he engaged the Penkethmans, had told them that Savage had inherited the house and all the contents, which must be well looked after but not disturbed. The Penkethmans, who innocently confided most of their gossip to Fowler when he called with the mail, told him this. Fowler's anxiety was about the contents of the safe. He'd got the fever which attacks those who partake in a gold rush. He could hardly control himself. He got that he could find no rest until he knew whether or not the fortune he dreamed about day and night was intact. The thought of thirty thousand pounds lying there to be taken became a phobia with him.'

Littlejohn paused. Fowler sat tight in his chair. The account so obviously tallied with most of his movements and thoughts of the past weeks that its unfolding struck him with terror.

'Then, at last, the great day arrived. The chance occurred. Fowler opened a letter from a lawyer to the Penkethmans making an appointment in connection with an inheritance due to Mrs. Penkethman. He was sure this greedy pair would let nothing keep them from it. He was right. At two o'clock that day, the coast was clear. No Sarah Rasp, no dogs, no Penkethmans. Fowler called with his letters at the farm and made sure they were out. Then he carefully let himself in *Johnsons Place*, put on his gloves and started to search. He went from room to room hunting for the safe, but he couldn't find it. He got in a frenzy and started to vent his spite on the furniture as though it were deliberately obstructing him. He opened drawers looking for some clue or other of where the money was hidden and strewed their contents around him. He even searched the beds. Then when he was almost at his wits' end, he remembered the cellar. He found the key and was starting to search down there when he was disturbed. The Savages had arrived.

'Fowler locked the cellar door and stood behind it waiting until the new arrivals went away. But Savage was determined to inspect every inch of his inheritance...'

Fowler suddenly leapt to his feet, his fists clenched and his teeth bared in a fearful grimace. He could hardly stand for rage. He seemed to be living through it all again. Then, suddenly he relaxed and looked at the men facing him with a pathetic gesture of appeal.

'Can you blame me? You say I was in a frenzy. What about Savage? He went absolutely berserk. Smashed the door down with a heavy chair and when he saw me there he just got me by the throat and started to strangle me. He wouldn't let me go. I had to hit him. He'd have killed me.'

'So, you did kill him...'

Fowler didn't seem to hear. He had suddenly thought of something.

'I want my lawyer.'

'Your lawyer's dead, I told you. But had he lived, he'd have done you no good. Mr. Cunliffe found the safe before you did. It was in an alcove in the cellar, he had a key, like you, and he removed the contents, thousands of pounds in cash, before you even found where it was hidden.'

Fowler gave in. He signed a statement which almost tallied with Littlejohn's account and went to gaol on a long sentence. If he behaves himself, he will be a free man again before he is too old to trouble the world with his renewed misdoings.

David Hubbard was found dead in his bed a week after Jeremiah Cunliffe's funeral. His hatred of the lawyer had kept him alive and when his enemy and rival of almost a lifetime no longer existed and his name had been discredited by his proved embezzlements, Hubbard had nothing more worth living for.

DEATH IN DESOLATION

GEORGE BELLAIRS

THE FARMHOUSE CRIMES

I t could almost be said that Littlejohn got involved in the
Farmhouse Murders by accident.

Throughout the spring and summer of 1965 the newspaper
headlines were monopolised by a series of carefully planned
crimes in farmhouses in remote areas. The first occurred in
Devonshire; the next in the Lake District; then in the Yorkshire
Dales. Each crime greatly distant from the last and the whole
country wondering where the next would happen.

The robberies were committed with a minimum of violence.
In most cases the victims were surprised at night, threatened,
tied-up and gagged with transparent tape and their cash... nothing
but cash... carried off. Once or twice, when the occupant showed
resistance or lack of co-operation, he was hit over the head.

The criminals had obviously made their plans carefully in
advance. They appeared mainly on local mart days, which termi-
nated after the banks had closed and left farmers with cash in
hand from cattle deals. There were three operators and they never
tackled any place with more than three people on the premises.
The raiders had been carefully described over and over again
from the start, but the details were of little help. They all wore

black nylon stockings over their heads and faces, with black gloves on their hands and rope-soled slippers of the foreign *espadrille* type on their feet.

They were a quick-moving lot. If there was a telephone to the place they visited, they cut the outside wires beforehand. If the farmer had a shotgun handy, one of them, who might have been a gymnast or a rugby player, was upon him in a flying tackle before he could use it. On one occasion only, when the victim had been too quick for the athlete, one of his companions had drawn a revolver and persuaded the farmer to hand over his own weapon. The leader was tall, thin and lithe, and attended to his business with speed and concentration; another, stocky and powerful, intent on overcoming scruples and resistance; the third was described as self-confident, almost cocky, a youngish man, nimble, slim and of medium height, who seemed to creep more than walk in a slimy sadistic way. They were all dressed in black trousers and sweaters and became known as the Black Lot.

After the unsolved sixth crime in Pembrokeshire, there was a terrific public outcry. Half the police of the country and most of the men in rural areas were out after them, but nobody could pretend to guard every isolated farmhouse against the intruders. Everybody was, as usual, asking what the police were doing about it, especially after the seventh crime, when The Creep, as the youngest of the trio had been called, shot and badly wounded a farmer who refused to be intimidated and snatched at his mask. Then only had the leader lost his temper and struck his companion a vicious blow across the mouth with the back of his gloved hand.

The police work had already been centralised under a Devon-shire Superintendent, Warlock, who had taken charge of the first of the investigations and whose energy and intelligence, although hitherto unsuccessful, had attracted the attention of his superiors. He had worked night and day until his efforts were cut short by a coronary attack which placed him in hospital for the rest of the summer. There, he received flowers with a 'Get Better Quickly' card on which were stuck with transparent tape four words clipped from a newspaper: *from the black lot.*

It was then that Littlejohn was appointed co-ordinator of the enquiry, and Cromwell was assigned to assist him.

Almost at once another crime, this time murder, was reported, at Sprawle Corner, a remote hamlet, near Marcroft, in Midshire.

When Littlejohn and Cromwell got out of the train at Rugby, Cromwell looked distastefully round the station.

'An aunt of mine, the black sheep of the family, once ran off with a porter she met on Rugby station and was never seen again,' he said, as if to himself.

There wasn't time for further details. Someone pushed his way through the crowd and dashed up to Cromwell.

'Chief Superintendent Littlejohn? I recognised you right away from your photos in the paper. My name's Crampitt, sir. Sergeant in the Midshire C.I.D. I've been sent to meet you. Rugby's not exactly in our manor and if the local boys had known you were coming, they'd have had the red carpet out...'

He cordially wrung Cromwell's hand and looked expectantly at Littlejohn, waiting to be introduced.

Littlejohn had difficulty in taking it seriously. Cromwell had to put his hand heavily on Crampitt's shoulder to stop the gush of his welcome.

'*This* is Chief Superintendent Littlejohn. My name's Cromwell.'

Crampitt wasn't in the least put out. He was young and resilient and wore a natty dark grey suit and a jaunty cloth hat with a feather in the band. He removed the hat and revealed a crew cut.

'I must have got you both mixed up. You were both in the picture in the paper, weren't you? This way.'

He led them through the milling crowds of travellers to a car standing in the forecourt of the station.

'Superintendent Taylor asked me to come and meet you both.

He's been detained on the Sprawle Corner murder. He'll be glad to see you. Superintendent Warlock was in charge of the farm crime cases, but his heart attack put an end to that. He's still on the sick list and we're having to improvise a bit...'

He had relieved them of their luggage and rammed it in the boot of the police car, still talking. They all climbed in the vehicle.

The sun was shining and the streets of Rugby were full of shoppers and cars. Crampitt drove quickly, but that didn't prevent his talking. Littlejohn filled and lit his pipe and Crampitt apparently took this as permission to smoke himself. After pulling up at traffic lights, he rapidly produced a small cheroot for himself and another for Cromwell and lit them both before the lights changed to green. The car filled with the opulent smell of cigars.

'We'll take the road through the country to Marcroft. It passes Sprawle. The scenery's nice, too.'

They might have been going on a picnic.

'Perhaps I'd better tell you a bit about the case, sir...'

He took the silence as consent and although they were travelling at sixty he rattled off his tale, speaking round the cheroot.

'Sprawle Corner's a strange place. There are three farms there and four houses and a Methodist chapel, all unoccupied, except one, Great Lands, where the dead man and his wife lived. His name was Quill.'

Crampitt coughed, opened the window and flung away his half-smoked cheroot impatiently as though it were choking him.

'The Quills were a queer lot. I was born not far from Sprawle and know about them. Harry Quill, the murdered man, was the last of the older generation and the last of the family who farmed Great Lands for centuries. He'd no children and I suppose his three nephews will inherit the farm, such as it is.'

'It's not much of a place, then?'

'Five hundred acres...'

'Not bad.'

'It *is* bad, though. Harry Quill was off his head. There were three farms there: Great Lands, with three hundred acres, and two others with about a hundred acres apiece. One of the small holdings was farmed by a chap called Seal; the other by a man of the name of Russell. A tractor overturned and killed Seal; Russell got drinking and went bust. Quill bought both farms, added the land to his own and let the farmhouses go derelict. The doors and anything else portable were soon pinched, the windows were all broken by hooligans and somebody even took slates off the roofs. The two farmhouses and a tied cottage that went with Isaac Seal's holding are just skeletons in ruins now.'

'But Quill farmed his five hundred acres?'

'That's just it. He didn't. He simply bought the two hundred acres and left them as they were – plus more than two hundred acres of his own. Almost the whole of the farm he allowed to go back to the wild.'

'Had he no stock?'

'A few sheep in the fields surrounding the house, that's all. The local agricultural committee took it up. They threatened what they'd do if he didn't put the land under cultivation again or else stock it, but they didn't seem to get very far. I don't know why. When you visit the farm, you'll see where all the five hundred acres, which had been salvaged from moorland at one time, are reverting to moorland again. You can see the wilderness encroaching like the tide coming in.'

He paused as though admiring his metaphors.

'What kind of a man was Harry Quill?'

'He was always odd and a bit of a recluse. A middle-sized man, fattish, with a red, clean shaven face when he *did* shave, and a shock of thick grey hair which looked as if it had never seen a comb. He always looked as if he'd robbed a scarecrow in his style of dress. No collar, a brass stud in the neckband of his shirt, and old clothes. He used to run into Marcroft now and then to do some shopping. He was always alone. His wife was an invalid. I heard she'd had polio when she was young and walked like somebody who'd had a stroke. She was Harry Quill's cousin and it's said he married her to keep the money in the family.'

'Was there money in the family, then?'

'That's a puzzle. After the murder, we had to go through the place and all the cash we found – his lawyer was with us to make matters regular – all the cash we found was about three pounds, four and ninepence halfpenny... I remember the halfpenny...'

'What had Mrs. Quill to say about it?'

'Not a thing. It seems Quill looked after all the money. With her being confined indoors, she never needed any cash and he never gave her any. There was no cheque book or bank passbook, no sign of invested savings... nothing. He either buried his cash or hid it in some safe place, or else the robbers found it and took it off with them. He used to pay his bills in cash and bought and sold odd items of stock now and then, so he must have had cash available more than we found...'

They arrived at a signpost which pointed from the trunk road to a narrower one. *Sprawle and Marcroft.*

The gradient gradually began to increase almost as soon as they left the highway and they snaked their way upwards to an acute corner with another sign: *Sprawle. Cul-de-sac.* They turned into a well-made road in which, however, two cars could only have passed with difficulty. Ditches along each side and tall bushes which cut off the view. Finally, the hedges thinned out and revealed the deserted hamlet which the murdered man, pursuing some crazy policy known only to himself, had denuded of inhabitants and left to go to rack and ruin.

To the left, the land fell slowly away in the direction of the highway they had just left. To the right the ground rose in barren fields enclosed in crumbling stone walls, to open moorland topped by a small hill covered in bracken and gorse. The fields themselves were a wilderness, clad alternately in rank brown grass and the bright green moss and foliage of undrained marshes. Ahead lay the silent deserted hamlet of Sprawle.

Crampitt reduced speed to a crawl to allow them to take it all in.

'Since they took Mrs. Quill to hospital this place has been deserted, except for police, newsmen and morbid sightseers. Even a few hours after the crime was discovered, you couldn't move for cars filled with people viewing the scene of the crime like a lot of vultures. In the end, we closed the road.'

They had arrived in the hamlet itself. The road passed through it and ended at a cluster of tumbledown cottages in the distance. Crampitt was still talking like a courier conducting a lot of excursionists.

'That clump of ruins at the end was once a community of crofters, who ran small farms – market gardens really – and sold their stuff on stalls at local markets. They packed up and went, one after another. They could earn better livings as roadmen, bus conductors and such like in the towns and have shops and cinemas on their doorsteps, instead of having to walk or cycle three or four miles every time they wanted a loaf or a bobbin of cotton...'

They came to the first buildings along the road, two small stone farmhouses set in narrow enclosures with old trees and bushes sadly hanging over ruined garden walls and outhouses.

'These are the two small farms I told you about. Lower Meadows and Lite's Corner.'

All the glass of the windows had been smashed by hooligans. The doors had been removed, too, and at Lower Meadows, which had a long corridor from front to back, they could see right through to the daylight beyond and the small derelict farmyard with a rotting mowing-machine in the middle of it. Half the slates of the Lite's Corner roof had been removed and the beams were bare. The small tied cottage adjoining Lite's ground had its front door nailed up. Someone had written across it *Joe loves Marlene* in paint which had once been white. The chimney had blown down and had crashed through the roof. In the overgrown front garden a torn-down, home-made sign. *Trespasers will be prosected.*

Crampitt increased speed a little and they continued their crawl along the road, which deteriorated as they progressed. Now, they bumped among the potholes and ruts and a line of grass appeared running down the middle of the broken asphalt. It was obvious that somewhere in the vicinity the Rural District Council ceased to be responsible for the road and that Quill or someone equally slovenly and parsimonious took over.

'Here we are. This is Great Lands.'

Crampitt pulled up and got out. His companions followed him, glad to limber up their limbs, stiffened in the police car too small for men of their dimensions. They all stood in front of the dilapidated farmhouse in contemplation. Crampitt leaned on the gate.

'Not much of a place, eh?'

Cromwell winked at Littlejohn behind Crampitt's back. The young detective, if such he could be called, seemed to have taken the initiative for the whole outing instead of, as instructed, simply being sent to meet them and conduct them to his superior officers. He was more like an estate agent showing them over a property and at the same time running it down because he didn't wish them to buy it.

'Must have been a nice place in its prime. Now just a tumble-down ruin.'

The farm was a massive place. Four up and four down, at least, stone built with a huge square front and broad steps ascending from a large desolate overgrown garden. In the rear they could see a series of substantial outbuildings providing a windbreak and protection for the house. The whole was surrounded by an impressive stone wall, broken by great gates in front and behind and could have been, in its heyday, completely shut off from the outside world, like those fortified Breton farmhouses strongly protected from the sea and especially from the marauders who came across it.

The front gates were open. The hinges were rusted, the wood rotten and they looked ready to collapse if you tried to move them. The beds of the front garden were covered in weeds and rank grass. At some time there must have been roses cultivated there, for there were briers, gone back to nature, rambling all over the place. Gaunt trees hung over it and the rotted leaves of past years covered the paths. A stone building, once perhaps a potting-shed, stood in one corner without a roof and from inside a tree had sprung and its trunk protruded through the spars.

'We'd better take a look over the place, just to give you some idea...'

Crampitt had brought the key with him and had unlocked the front door. They all entered.

Every house has its own peculiar smell and that of this place wasn't at all pleasant. The Quills had lived alone, the woman had been an invalid. Presumably the house had been neglected. They knew that as soon as they stepped in the hall. The kitchens, drains, damp walls and carpets, the abandonment of every effort to keep the place properly clean all contributed their share to the tainted air, shut in behind closed windows. Above all there was one dominating odour...

'Have there been some cats shut up in here?' asked Littlejohn, puffing hard at his pipe.

It seemed to remind Crampitt that he ought to counter the complaint and he took out another cheroot, handed one to Cromwell and lit them both.

'There were four cats. After Mrs. Quill and her husband's body were taken away, the cats must have been locked in. They must have hidden somewhere. We had to get the R.S.P.C.A. along to dispose of them. They were all old and helpless...'

They passed from room to room of the forlorn farmhouse. It

was like a dream world, a fantastic scene from a gothic novel. Two only of the rooms seemed to have been used. The large kitchen and a small adjoining room used as a bedroom. The former was cheaply furnished with a large rough table on which the remnants of a meal, spread on old newspapers instead of a cloth, still remained. A couple of plain wooden chairs, drawn up, as their occupants had left them before the tragedy. A rocking-chair and a saddleback upholstered in horsehair at the fireside; a large plain wooden dresser along one side, with a motley assortment of crockery arranged on the shelves.

There were no modern amenities. The kitchen was flagged and the damp stone added to the general smell of the place. Pieces of matting here and there. A stone sink with a large brass tap. The fireplace with an oven on each side was huge and blackleaded. Any hot water seemed to have been drawn from a boiler at one side. The dead remains of a small fire in the grate and two dirty pans on the hob. Great empty hooks in the beams where perhaps hams had hung in better times.

In modern days, how could such a place exist?

The rest of the house was even worse. Like a caricature of the castle of the Sleeping Beauty in which everybody has fallen asleep and dust and cobwebs had slowly obliterated all signs of normal habitation. The bedroom, with the soiled linen and a patchwork quilt jumbled on the huge, brass-knobbed double bed, just as they had been left after the crime. A chest of drawers, a cane-bottomed chair and two large cheap wardrobes, which emitted a blast of mothballs when they opened them and which contained a motley confused assortment of men's and women's clothes, moth-ridden and rotting on their hooks.

The rest of the rooms had not been used for years; some might not even have been entered. Several were bare; others contained odds and ends of furniture, all dirty, the good and the junk all indiscriminately thrown together. Now and then, they came across something unusual, something which had been beautiful, perhaps treasured once and had its period of delight.

Littlejohn felt stupefied by the mess around him and began to wonder vaguely what they were doing there at all. Crampitt was leaning against the door-frame of the kitchen, his cheroot still in the corner of his mouth, looking slightly pleased with himself, as though he were giving the other two a new type of experience, the kind they didn't encounter in their investigations in London.

'I think we've seen enough.'

Littlejohn wanted a breath of fresh air after it all.

'Let's go outside and you can tell us the facts of the case.'

Crampitt nodded and looked pleased.

'Our men have been all over the lot with a fine-tooth comb. The robbers didn't leave any traces. Nor was there anything to help with the enquiry. As I said, very little money was left. You haven't seen the dairy at the back of the kitchen. It's got a lot of old corroded equipment in it, but it hasn't been used for years. Same with the outbuildings. A lot of accumulated rubbish...'

After all, the local police were concerned with the ruins and the rubbish. Littlejohn made for the front door without more ado and stepped into the open air again. There was a fine view of the flat countryside below with the trunk roads full of traffic passing along the bottom of the slope. And Quill and his wife had retreated to their tumbledown house, shut themselves away from civilisation and allowed the rest of their world to rot and tumble about their ears.

'This is briefly how it happened...'

Crampitt was at it again.

'... Yesterday morning, a man passing on the main road from Rugby to Marcroft stopped a police car and said a farm on the hillside was on fire and he showed them the smoke billowing in the distance. It was this place, Great Lands. The alarm was given and the fire brigade and local police were soon on the spot...'

'Yes,' said Littlejohn, watching a hawk hovering over the hill-side below.

'When they arrived here, they found someone had set fire to an old haystack in the farmyard...'

Cromwell looked up suddenly.

'A haystack in a farmyard!'

'Yes. If you don't believe me, take a look. It's still there, burnt out. You have to remember, this wasn't an ordinary farm. It was run by a madman. That's what I think. Quill was a madman.'

'Go on...'

Crampitt looked as if he expected an apology from Cromwell for interrupting. None came. He continued.

'It was thought that Mrs. Quill had fired it to attract attention. What else could she do? No phone, unable to walk any distance, nobody about. They found her on the doorstep, collapsed. She'd had a stroke. It took her speech and one side of her body. She's in Marcroft Hospital and she hasn't spoken a word since they found her. Until she speaks, or at least, shows any interest in what's going on, nobody will quite know what happened.'

'What about her husband?'

'I'm coming to that. They found him in the kitchen doorway, dead, with his wife beside him. He'd been killed by a blow on the back of his head. You'll see the pathologist's report at headquarters. The crime had probably been committed the night before between eight and ten o'clock. Mrs. Quill must have been left with the body for the whole night and until ten the next morning, when the fire at the farm was spotted. I suppose she was wondering how to get help. How she made her way from the house to the far side of the farmyard to fire the stack, God alone knows. She could hardly walk a yard.'

'Any traces of whoever committed the crime?'

'None whatever. Of course, that's the way the Black Lot work, isn't it?'

'You're sure it was the Black Lot.'

'Well, in view of what's been going on lately, we naturally

assumed it was another of their crimes. It follows the pattern of the rest, doesn't it?'

'That remains to be seen. I suppose the results of the investigation so far will be on file at headquarters?'

'Yes. There's quite a big file, but, so far, it hasn't been of much help. Unless Mrs. Quill recovers consciousness and has something spectacular to tell us, it looks as if the Quill crime will join the rest of the Black Lot ones...'

Cromwell interrupted him.

'How long did you say you've been in the police, Sergeant Crampitt?'

'Ten years.'

'H'm.'

Crampitt didn't seem in any way affected by the hint. He led the way back to the police car.

'That be all for now?'

'For the present, yes, Crampitt,' said Littlejohn. 'We'd better report at headquarters and see what they have to say...'

When they arrived at headquarters in Marcroft, they were told that Mrs. Quill had died an hour ago without recovering consciousness.

Join the

GEORGE BELLAIRS
READERS' CLUB

And get your next
George Bellairs Mystery free!

When you sign up, you'll receive:

1. A free classic Bellairs mystery, *Corpses in Enderby*;

2. Details of Bellairs' new publications and the opportunity to get copies in advance of publication; and,

3. The chance to win exclusive prizes in regular competitions.

Interested?

It takes less than a minute to join. Just go to

www.georgebellairs.com

to sign up, and your free eBook will be sent to you.